W9-BZC-222

Pacifist Chicken
And Other
Largely Humorous
Stories of small Hopes

Andrea Kampic

Copyright ©2005 by Andrea Kampic
Photography ©2005 by Andrea Kampic

All rights reserved. No part of this publication may be reproduced, stored in a
retrieval system or transmitted in any form or by any means whether electronic,
mechanical, photocopying, recording or otherwise, without the prior written
permission of the publisher.

Published by
Blue Agave Press
Los Angeles, California
www.kampictures.com

The characters and events in this book are fictitious and figments of the
author's imagination. Any resemblance to actual events or persons is one of
those crazy life coincidences.

ISBN 0-9767909-3-9
Library of Congress Control Number (LCCN): 2005906875

First Blue Agave Press paperback printing April 2006

Art Direction and Cover Design by Robert Randall
All Photography by Andrea Kampic

Printed in the United States of America on recycled, acid-free paper.

BLUE
AGAVE

PRESS

Acknowledgements

This book would be quite different (read: rubbish) if not for contributions from many friends. I greatly appreciate all the input from the following for their individual gifts, encouragement, and their generous expenditures of time. For early draft reading and comments: Karen Erbach (the earliest), John Richards, Eric Moore, Carole Zakkour (also came up with the 'small hopes' tagline), Andrea Keldsen, Kimber Hightower, Sue Harvey, Genevieve Coleman, Tom Blanton, Robert Randall, Brian Erbach (for lots of love, as well as tech support and patience), Andrew McKenzie, Maria Bennett, Ginny Bishop (also PR/marketing expertise), Alice Hogge and Betty Swartz. For cover design, art direction and all around watching-my-back, great thanks to Robert Randall. For some much needed, easy-to-swallow editing, Terri Sota (multi-talented Terri also helped with marketing). For the game show idea in What's Your Problem?, thanks to Julie Pozatek Weiner. Finally, for inspiration, thanks to all the artists and writers and photographers and performers and musicians and activists and everyday innovators putting their work out there for us to inhale.

For my dad, Willis Kampic.
He made me laugh.

Contents

My Dream Dog

I know this will shock some people, it sort of shocks me now, much later, when I can see clearly, but a few years ago I fell in love with my dog. He was everything I was looking for in a mate. He was tall, when he stood on two legs, and very handsome; had plenty of hair; was always interested in what I was doing and really listened when I talked about my day; was up for anything, at any time; was happy to run errands with me; never complained; gratefully ate anything I fed him; seemed to really appreciate me; was protective of me; liked staying home and just watching a movie on a Saturday night; never drank or did drugs; was happy to meet my friends and was always respectful and kind to them; had no religious or political views that I disagreed with (I suspected he was a liberal like me after listening to so much NPR); missed me when I was at work, and was so happy to see me when I came home. This was all I was looking for and there he was, my daily companion. How could I not fall for him?

We met when a friend introduced us at a party at his house. This friend had found Charlie, my dog, on the street a few days before. Charlie had cuts on his paws and was very skinny and desperately in need of a place to live and a few good meals. I had just moved into my new house a few months before, and well, I just wanted Charlie right then and there. I took him home that night and we've been together ever since. Charlie was a bit young for me—I was looking for someone more mature—but you take what you can get.

Well, we got along great right away. Charlie was fun and lively and with him, there was always some welcome distraction from my work and responsibilities. He had some issues with chewing on things, but I was patient and didn't yell and respected this stage in his growth so we got through it. He rarely made a mess, in fact, I'd been with many men who were much sloppier and cleaned themselves far less often than Charlie. Charlie was different. He often picked up his toys and carried them around with him. He used the same bowl every day, rarely needed to be brushed, never needed a trim, was just plain low-maintenance. When Charlie needed his space, well, he just went off by himself in another room, no fuss about it, no scene. When he had to go out, he let me know and I opened the door for him. After a while, I just left the back door open so he didn't have to ask; this wasn't kindergarten.

He was very dark and foreign. He was part German shepherd and part Labrador retriever. I believe Labrador is some exotic island. That's where he got his playfulness, I surmised. The German part was the clean and tidy bit. Overall, this made a good mix and I recommend it for anyone seeking a companion. He had dark hair and a long face. His body was lean, but muscular. He ate a lot, but never seemed to gain weight. Oh, and he was a terrific athlete. What a jumper! I taught him to catch the frisbee and he was excellent at it right from the start. He could leap three feet off the ground to catch it and was so proud of himself when he did. He would strut around the yard for a minute, daring me to come get it from him, but I learned that if I didn't go after him, he would bring it back for me to throw again. At these moments, I just couldn't believe that he had been dumped so unceremoniously in the street. Who would let a good one like this go, I wondered, but then remembered that it takes all kinds.

It was very hard to go to work and leave him all day, especially at first. We missed each other terribly, and sometimes I would even come home from work to have lunch with him, but then I had to leave him twice in a day, and that was even harder. He would get that tragic, "I'm being abandoned again" look and I just hoped he knew I was coming back and would never abandon him. I left the radio on all day and I would call and leave messages on the answering machine so that he could hear my voice periodically throughout the day. When I came home, that was wonderful. I rarely made plans to see my friends after I got him; I would rather be with Charlie. They said that it wasn't healthy for me, but I disagreed and reminded them that he had been abandoned, didn't they have any compassion?

Charlie and I communicated intuitively, and I never felt the barrier of his not being able to speak back to me. A good listener is more important than a good talker to me, since I'm a bit of a talker. I told him my secrets, things I knew he would, well could, never repeat. When I felt sad, he stayed close by my side, looking at me with sympathetic eyes. Just his presence was often enough to make me snap out of it. I mean, what did I really have to be so sad about? He reminded me that I had a lot. And when I was happy, he sensed that too. He would wag his tail and bark and jump up on his hind legs and I would hold his head next to mine and it would make both of us happy. We were very close.

He slept in the bed with me. That started the first night he came home with me, I'm ashamed to admit. He was just so cute and snuggly, and jumped right up like he belonged there, so I didn't have the heart to stop him. He snored a bit, but I've been told that I do too, so who was I to complain? Sometimes he would wake up in the middle of the night scared from a nightmare or he would jump up barking at some noise outside. This sort of scared me, at first, but after a while we both got used to the occasional disruptions and would both fall right back asleep.

We laughed a lot, well, I did, and I think he laughed in his own way too. I like a good sense of humor, and when someone can make me laugh, heck, that's half the battle right there. And he was always doing something funny, that Charlie. The way he looked like he was talking when he chewed on a bone or a cookie; the way he crossed his paws when he lay next to me on the floor; the way he threw a ball up in the air with his nose and caught it on the way down, amusing himself for long stretches of time without any help from me. It was all hours of pleasure and happiness for me, my time with Charlie.

After a series of terrible dates and short turbulent relationships, I had become pretty discouraged about men around this time in my life. When Charlie came along, I had just about given up on finding someone to spend my life with, maybe have children with, a companion. Charlie fulfilled so many of those needs that I nearly forgot that I was lonely and needed to find someone. But after a time, those thoughts came back to me and I became depressed. I didn't want to go out at night and leave Charlie home by himself, and there was no one interesting at work and the few men that my friends had fixed me up with were embarrassing, I mean, is that what they think of *me?* So anyway, one night, I was crying in bed before I went to sleep, and Charlie came up and licked my face and lay next to me and put his head on the pillow next to mine and I spooned him and I just wished so much that Charlie was a man. A human man. Just the way he was, his personality and his temperament, but in the body of a man. I would never wish for anything again, I swore. I would be happy for the rest of my life. It would be my dream come true I thought as I cried myself to sleep.

I slept fitfully and woke the next morning to find Charlie's warm body curled up against my back. As I reached around to pet him and stroke his stomach, something felt weird. Really weird. I turned and looked and screamed at the half-awake man lying in my bed. I pulled back the covers, exposing his chest and lower torso, all naked, and ran to find Charlie. Why hadn't he warned me? Something terrible must have happened to Charlie. "Charlie!" I cried.

As I grabbed my robe and was running from the room, I heard

a throat clear and then a strange, but calm and controlled voice say, "I'm right here." I whipped around and saw Charlie's eyes on this man's face as he tried awkwardly to sit up in my bed. I blinked. I blinked again. He *did* sort of look like Charlie, but, I pinched myself hard on the arm. It hurt and I didn't wake up. That can only mean that there is a god and I was awake. I walked slowly toward the bed, not taking my eyes off of this oddly familiar stranger. "I feel a little strange today," he said. "Maybe I'm sick."

"How can you be Charlie? You, well, you're not a dog."

"I don't know what you mean," he said, not seeming to understand that he had changed. I sighed, went over to my side of the bed and poked his chest. He was very hairy. He leaned toward me with his tongue out. I jerked away from him. "What's wrong? I was just going to lick your face."

"Charlie, if you really are Charlie and not some hallucination I conjured, you are freaking me out. Give me a minute."

"Okay, but I gotta pee." He jumped off the bottom of the bed and landed loudly, all splayed on the floor, completely naked. Before I could try to help, or truly take in his naked butt, he had righted himself, and limped slightly out the door. I put my head in my hands. Then, all of a sudden getting a nasty mental picture, I ran toward the bathroom and arrived just in time to see him trying to raise his leg and pee into the toilet while standing directly over it. "This isn't so easy."

"Well, that's not how it's done, actually. You just stand straight in front of it, and well, you have to hold it, no, touch it like this and point it toward the hole there, and, you know, aim it." I turned away, embarrassed.

I went into the living room and sat down, giving him his privacy while taking a moment for myself. Could this really be Charlie, my dog? I *had* wished very hard the night before for just this, but dreams like that just don't come true. They're against nature, and I knew that when I wished it. But I had never thought, in a million years, even if I had been very devout, which I wasn't, that this was how things would be in my house when I awoke this morning. Just then, the naked man calling himself Charlie walked into the living room and lay down on the floor in a loud thump. "Ouch," he said. I walked over to him and pulled him up by his hand and said, "Let's find you something to wear."

In the back of my closet was a bag full of clothes from the various men I had known, some left in their haste to depart, others I may have taken from them as souvenirs. I pulled the bag out while "Charlie" stood there, full frontal, and watched. I removed a pair of jeans and a sweatshirt. Avoiding staring at his penis, which looked human all right, I opened a dresser drawer and found an extra large t-shirt, and I pulled a pair of men's briefs that I wore sometimes from my underwear drawer. I handed them to him. He just stood there. I smiled, realizing that I was going to have to dress him. I talked to him, describing how each article fit and he helped a little as I slipped them on. "But why do I have to wear these things?" Charlie wanted to know.

"You don't see me walking around naked do you?"

"Sometimes," he said, which was true, and made me feel oddly, uncomfortably spied upon by this man/dog.

"Yeah, but most of the time I wear clothes, right?"

"But I don't," Charlie pointed out.

"Just humor me" was all I could muster.

We walked into the kitchen. Well, I walked and Charlie followed right on my heels, literally. "I guess you must be hungry," I managed to find some words.

"Starved, just like every morning." Okay, how odd is this, I thought as I cracked a few eggs for me and Charlie, formerly known as my dog. I just had to accept this, I thought to myself as Charlie sat down heavily on the floor. I mean, however it happened, he was clearly a man now.

Suddenly, in a wicked flash, I saw things a little differently. I smiled to myself. I turned on NPR and showed Charlie how to sit in a chair and it dawned on me that this felt really good, a morning with a man without the awkwardness after the night before. No strings attached, no waiting for him to say he'll call, no bullshit.

"Hey, Charlie, you want to take a walk in the park this morning?"

"Do I ever," he said and his tongue came out of his mouth. This could be fun, I thought as I served Charlie his first meal as a human being.

Well, the first few days were an adjustment, that's for sure: teaching Charlie how to use utensils, and how to drink from a glass, which he had a lot of trouble with, and trimming his fingernails, and bathing, and standing up straight, and watching TV, and answering the telephone and sitting on the couch with his legs, not his arms, on the floor. He laughed for the first time when we watched TV and a cat food commercial came on with a really spoiled cat that ignored its owner because it was simply too finicky to eat the commercial food it was given. He laughed like a hyena. But Charlie was so pleased with himself that he understood the concept, well, he mentioned it again and again after that. He tried several times to sniff my crotch, which was very disconcerting, and the butt sniffing habit was especially hard to break. But he caught on quick and I was just damn glad I had waited to have him neutered.

Going to work was very hard because I worried what he could get into and how he could harm himself because he didn't know, well, anything. I gave him a crash course in the stove and the iron and the scary stuff and made sure he understood about not opening the door or going outside until I came home. He seemed to understand, but I called about twenty times a day. My friends at work wondered what kind of guy would tolerate that kind of nagging and checking up on, but I just laughed and said 'new relationship' as if that explained everything.

After a few days of this, I was exhausted by the way, I came home from work and the door was open and Charlie was not home. I panicked. I ran down the street calling his name, every horrible fear running through my head, much worse than if he had been a runaway dog, and I saw him up the street talking to a woman. Just then, he started humping her leg. She slapped him and hit him with her purse and he jumped back, dejected. I ran up to him and grabbed his sweatshirt and spun him around. He had that same look I remembered from his dog days when I was sad, but now he was sad. "She hit me," he cried.

"Charlie, you can't leave the house without me. You don't know how to behave yet. And I already told you about the humping. Did you forget?"

"What's forget?" he asked and I had no answer.

"Don't hump," I said. "Don't leave the house."

"But it's boring," he said.

"How much more boring can it be than when you were a dog?" I asked. "At least now you can watch TV and fix yourself a snack and talk to me on the phone. This has to be better."

"I didn't know it was boring then. I just didn't know any better." He wanted to see the world. I could see it in his eyes. What could I do? I had to take him out to meet my friends and go to the movies and take him to the inside of a grocery store and show him a museum and fine art and a rock concert (we had to leave because it hurt his ears) and buy him some new clothes and let him ride in the front seat of the car.

It was so cute when Charlie was a dog and he stuck his head out of the window and let his tongue fly around, the wind whipping his hair. It's not so cute when your boyfriend does it. Some of my friends thought he was handsome, others wondered where in the world I found him since he was so odd. I told them we met at the dog park. He wasn't so odd to me anymore because I was used to him, but I'm sure he seemed it to them. My friends wondered what had happened to Charlie, the dog, and I said that he had run away, and wasn't it a funny coincidence that I met Charlie the man around the same time. They wondered why I didn't seem more upset about my dog, but I said I was very upset inside and couldn't even bring myself to talk about it, which was really true.

Charlie was a terribly sloppy eater, and ate so fast that I'm sure he didn't taste anything. He had large, hairy hands, which started to look like a werewolf's to me as time went on. He still jumped up and ran to the door when I came home, which used to be really cute, but now it disturbed me. I wanted him to have his own life. He was lazy and laid around all the time. He slept until noon most days also, so it seemed almost like he was depressed (maybe he was for all he knew) or that's just the dog in him. He couldn't cook, couldn't pay for anything, but believe me he could eat, which got expensive.

It became uncomfortable with my friends when we would go out because I would always drive and pay. They started to call and say that they didn't care that he was between jobs, he needed to be giving me money, and then I started to lie and tell them that he was. I said he was writing a novel.

The irony in that was that he couldn't even read, which was a huge problem because I loved to read and talk about things I have read and he couldn't bring anything to our discussions unless it could be gleaned from TV or picture magazines.

He still jumped up in the middle of the night, which drove me crazy, because he scared the crap out of me and I couldn't go back to sleep afterward like I used to. It's very creepy to see a grown man leap up and sniff the air and run around the room making grunting noises.

We were no longer able to communicate intuitively, which may be the thing I missed most of all. Once spoken language was introduced, and since English wasn't his first language actually, he lost that great cool thing he had with his expressions and his eyes. He came to rely on the words, and he only knew about one thousand of them, so that's definitely a limited way to communicate.

I'd love to send him to college, have him learn a skill so he could work and not be so bored, but like I said he couldn't read. And I'm sure that he could've learned, but I thought it might have put me over some abyss, driving my boyfriend because he didn't have a car or know how to drive to adult school because he couldn't read.

I used to fantasize that he was a liberal and I did my best by leaving the radio on, but he didn't even know what politics meant or literature or art or themes or metaphors or the internet or PBS. Again, this limited what we could talk about. He broke a tooth playing frisbee the first day we tried to rekindle that fun, so that was the end of that. He still scratched himself in public, but he no longer tried to lick his balls, thank goodness. Basically, things he was interested in, me mostly, just weren't that interesting, even to me.

It all came down to this: I wanted my dog back. I truly missed my dog. I longed for those days with Charlie, how happy we were, thinking with self-pity that I could have found some man *and* kept my dog. Now I had a half-man/half-dog and not a whole one of either. Slowly, at night, I started to pray for Charlie, my dog, to be in bed with me the next morning when I woke up.

I'm ashamed to say this, but I even left him one day at the park. When he went to pee in the bushes, I ran to the car and drove away, but I saw him coming out of the woods and the look on his face and remembering he had been abandoned and that really, deep down he was Charlie my dog, and it was my fault that he was trapped in this wrong life, well, I turned around and picked him up and didn't say a word. But he could see that I had tried to ditch him and the hurt in his face was beyond words. I promised myself that I would never do that again but still kept praying before I went to bed. But he didn't change back. Each morning I eagerly looked to see, but it was a man that greeted me with a cheery smile and a face lick, not my dog.

I couldn't go on like this I thought. I couldn't confide in anyone, couldn't consult a website anonymously for a chat room, or search the Merck Manual for a cure or find a self help group, because nothing like this existed anywhere. I was trapped in this nightmare for, I feared, forever. We didn't go out anymore. He didn't understand movies, a play was out of the question and my friends had come to think I could do *much* better. On those occasions that we needed to get out of the house, I would just drive around and let him stick his head out the window. I secretly hoped that he would get bored or lonely or cabin fever or something and want to leave, but he never mentioned it. He sat quietly next to me if I read or watched TV, if I talked on the phone he would look out the window, if I went out without him he was happy to see me pull in the driveway. Somebody innocently, casually, the other day mentioned be careful what you wish for and I burst into tears.

So now, I make the best of it. We've settled into a routine

together. He's learned how to make the bed and sometimes, with supervision, I let him use the stove. We took a trip to the mountains recently and he was so darn happy running in the woods that it was almost okay for a day. It could be worse, I tell myself, but when I try to articulate it, I can't imagine how.

And then last week I missed my period.

Modern Primitives

The Geniuses in Marketing had done it again. They were going to put IBMMicrohard in the spin cycle and we were finally going to come out clean.

It had been a rough few years. Stock in The Company was way down after the series of accounting scandals. Then the media found out how much the board was paying the new tough-talking, across-the-board-budget-cutting CEO and he had to be fired to prevent a riot. Then the public found out that we were the ones that had sabotaged our competitors through the e-mail 'Smile' worm. Everyone in The Company had stock in The Company, and we were all hurting. Morale was very low since this is how most of us lived day-to-day; selling stock regularly to pay for our outlandish lifestyles. We were encouraged to live lavishly since the Guys Upstairs thought if we looked prosperous, it might reflect well on The Company in general. Now we were selling so we wouldn't be suckers. And they just kept giving us more, in lieu of pay raises, which created a sort of internal inflation so our shares were becoming more and more worthless. Most of the lawsuits were settled now, with no one actually going to jail, but surprisingly, people just hadn't let bygones be bygones. And our newest ad campaign slogan 'Buy Now, Pay Later' had been a complete failure.

But things were changing thanks to Marketing. Gruel Fibbons, the famous and highly trusted Naturalist, Nutritional Guru and Television Personality (who also happens to be heavily in hock my friends in accounting tell me, but I'm not supposed to repeat that), has signed on for the stunt we were going to pull. It was a stroke of pure perfection in pairing: embattled IBMMicrohard publicly challenging Gruel Fibbons to live in the wild for sixty days, without benefit of any technological device, nor any modern convenience. Of course, Gruel was pretty soft around the middle and didn't even eat his own menus of mush and bran, so he will fail and return from the wild early, having been sustained all along by The Company so he can make it say, forty-five days to save face, and then, humbled, he will extol the merits of modern technology to the world. Technology had been getting a bad rap and Marketing figured it was just a matter of putting the right face on it: Gruel's. You see, the world had gone the other way of late, turning its back on all of the wonderful things that The Company and a select few others have provided, biting the hand that feeds it so to speak, and we needed to create The Want again, whether the ingrates really need it or not. You know things are not right in the world when the Unabomber is released from prison due to an outcry of public sympathy and corporate Captains of Industry are being jailed for mere malfeasance.

So, Gruel, as he is known worldwide, was game. He balked at first, pretending to have scruples, but when large carrots of the monetary kind were dangled he saw the brilliance of The Plan. Plus, his star was setting anyway and the publicity would be priceless. We envisioned several TV cameras, planted strategically, to expertly show what it is that Gruel will be doing whenever we tell him to do something. 'Gruel, rub some berries on your chin to look like you just ate some!' 'Gruel, turn camera left and give us your better side while you peel that bark and look for grubs!' That sort of thing. He will be having his hair done daily to make him look 'woodsy' and his wardrobe will be chosen carefully from among our designer corporate sponsors. The idea is to make it look 'natural' (even The Company calls the components in its computer products 'natural plastic' to capitalize on the trend).

We had location scouts already searching for a nice spot near a stream, where we could shoot without having any houses or power lines or freeways nearby, which is harder than you might think. They've been looking at Northern Montana, but we would have to do that in mid-summer otherwise Gruel's agent said Gruel won't do it. Even at that time of year Gruel was concerned about cold weather (he's from LA), but we assured him he would have an electric heater in his tent and cashmere socks. So, the idea is, we find the spot, set it all up to look 'real' and figure we'll have a captive audience for forty-five days, the anticipation building daily to see if he'll make it; he won't, people will be sad and disappointed and will then have to question the merits of the whole 'natural' movement and speculate on how much longer Gruel could have gone if he had only had a GPS system and a palm pilot with a built in topographical map and an IBMMicrohard bluetooth computer for the instantaneous look-up of poisonous plants and modern Gore-Tex insulated gear or even a gun for god's sake for when we bring out the circus bear (we have Smith and Wesson and Winchester already signed on for stealth sponsorship, which has become huge in The Biz).

The only real concern was Gruel himself. Besides the rumors that he was looney tunes, no one thought he could act. I mean, several billion people worldwide needed to be convinced that he was actually eating bugs and bark and 'roughing it' for forty-five days. He had been taking acting lessons from some of the best in The Business for several days now, but he just wasn't coming along fast enough. The fear is that all this money and talent will be built around the shaky franchise of Gruel Fibbons. They had a few more weeks of intense hype before he was to actually go to Montana or wherever, but my sources were deeply concerned. They had him watch *The Blair Witch Project* over and over to prepare him for the sense of fear they want him to project, especially at night when they let loose one of the trained animals by his tent, and he'd also been watching some of the rehearsal tapes to force him to view his own twitches and grimaces and insincere gestures. No one could believe that they had not been pointed out to him before, so we figure he must be surrounded by Yes-Men, which was something we could all understand. Gruel felt that the public responded to his 'unscripted' moments, but our focus groups have proven him dead wrong. He had been boning up on his edible plant knowledge, even though he knew that the noted botanist Herb Johnston would be behind the camera for the entire ordeal, showing which plants he could eat and giving him quick blurbs about them in remedial English that he could share with the viewing audience. Gruel said he wanted it to feel 'authentic.' We all nodded our heads like he had a point there, but in private, we mocked him mercilessly. He just seemed unstable to those of us in Image Management and we certainly expressed our collective concerns to Upper Management in our weekly The-Job-You-Save-May-Be-Your-Own Meeting. But he was the only one with the motivation, the credentials and the on-camera experience. So, Gruel it was.

The days leading up to D-Day (short for Dupe and having something to do with that big war a really long time ago) ticked by very quickly for those of us in The Company involved with *Can Gruel Survive?* The Media Blitz cost a fortune, but research shows you have to lay it on thick at the very beginning to hook your viewers' asses to their barcaloungers. Time slots are highly competitive and very scary places.

Montana proved simply too rugged, so we chose a few acres on Harrison Ford's property in Wyoming. Ford also needed the money, being a grandfather now, so it was a win/win for everyone. And his own house was set far enough back in the woods that there were very few angles we had to be careful with (the tin roof reflected intensely at certain times of day, but our cameraman assured us he could work around it). We're all professionals here, after all.

Well, the anticipation was just intense. We had already received letters from as far away as Florida congratulating us on the concept. We installed 2500 high-tech instant transmittal ratings devices in 2500 receptive (read: bought and paid for) families' homes to give us the data we needed to show the media to prove the popularity of Gruel's show. He was at that moment on the Lear jet to take him to the property. We had already shot the opening credits and the first show where he is 'dropped' from a helicopter (it's actually a nearly identical looking stunt double in a fab wig) into the rugged wilderness (Locations found some actual rugged wilderness in Canada for these overheads). Gruel's contract stipulated that he was not to actually be in the wilderness as he was agoraphobic but Marketing thought the helicopter would be daring and pull the audience in immediately by setting up Gruel as a risk-taker and all around Genuine Guy. We did the close-ups with Gruel looking lost and scared upon landing and Editing said it was good enough for TV. We had to set him up as feeble right away so we wouldn't get too much hate mail during his inevitable failure in the end. It's called foreshadowing in The Biz.

Gruel was allowed to bring three books by our Contest Advisory Board and he chose an obscure essay by Joe Knowles called 'Alone in the Wilderness' from like, the last century, which we thought was brilliance incarnate since it made him look well-read and historically hip while still being vulnerable and conscientious; 'Ulysses' since it was on some list as the best book ever written and Gruel wanted to seem intellectual and in-the-know (plus it was nearly a thousand pages and he had a lot of time to kill), and the latest John Grisham political thriller to lure in the pop culture audience, and besides Grisham's publisher was a Sponsor and Subsidiary. Gruel actually could have had whatever books he wanted at any time, but he said that he wanted to add some integrity to the show so until he said otherwise, no other books were allowed on the set. One of my Team Tasks was to read the Joe Knowles essay and synopsize it for Upper Management, since we knew sales would skyrocket and Legal wanted to make sure it wasn't subversive.

Well, the initial shows were a great success. The ratings were through the roof, and not just the rigged ones. Inexplicably, we had ourselves a show horse, as we say in The Biz. IBMMicrohard's stock started to soar upward again, filling us all once again with dreams of bigger and grander lifestyles. It felt like the Old Days. Gruel's acting lessons seemed to have paid off as he alternated between confident, experienced Woodsman/Naturalist and mildly fearful Respecter of Nature. These were his only two personas actually, but the public was eating it up. There were betting pools in Vegas as to whether he would make it and if not, how many days he would last. In between shooting, Gruel would eat cheese and crackers at the craft service table and often took his lunch with the crew. They found him to be affable, but a bit of a know-it-all, and since they all knew it was a total stunt, this didn't go over very well. But the crew was sworn to secrecy, and anyone who spilled the beans would be blackballed for life from the lucrative Reality Entertainment Business, so that kept them in line.

Then things subtly started to change. Actually, it was Gruel who started to change. He picked up that Joe Knowles book and as he read, he started to figure he could really make it sixty days on his own and he didn't need The Network to coddle him—he was a Naturalist after all—he could do this alone since others before him had succeeded, why not him too? He forgot that the entire show was about his failing and proving the deep-seeded need among human beings for the Technological rather than the Natural and that The Network wasn't going to allow this substantive change in their show's content. But Gruel, a trifle but not a fool, realized that he actually was the show. And it was too popular for them to pull its plug.

He began to refuse to eat lunch and wandered off, sending the camera crew scrambling to do hand-held 'on location' work following him through the woods and trying to avoid capturing the houses in the distance. He actually started to peel back bark and asked Johnston, who was always off-camera (now running to keep up, and he was even older than Gruel), which grubs were edible (it turns out they all are, who knew?). He ate mushrooms that he picked along the way, and sautéed them in duck fat from a duck that he caught with a homemade spear (it was an extremely lucky throw). He made those mmmmmmm sounds as he ate the mushrooms as if they were the best things he had ever eaten. Sales of mushrooms skyrocketed after that episode.

But as you can imagine, The Company did not care if mushroom sales were brisk if Modern Technology was still demonized, regardless of the fact that mushrooms were also one of the show's sponsors. They instructed The Network to put the pressure on Gruel's hapless agent, who made numerous desperate cell phone calls to Fibbons, pleading with him to relent and follow his contract. Tired of his self-serving groveling, Gruel fired him. Somehow he realized that this was his last chance to redeem himself from the lies that had been his life. Gruel discovered that there had always been a dark cloud over Joe Knowles regarding his sojourn in the wilderness and questions remained as to whether it was actually rigged by the newspaper that followed the story way back when, but Gruel chose to wholeheartedly believe that he himself could do it, even if Knowles had been weak.

So, The Company had no choice but to fight back. They instructed Herb Johnston to give Gruel, whom we were now all instructed to call The Prima Donna, false information and encourage him to eat things that would make him sick. Consequently, he spent nearly an entire episode throwing up. The Company was very happy about this and carefully placed opinion pieces written by various scientists, including Johnston, in several Op/Ed sections of Major Newspapers about the unlikelihood of anyone actually living in the wilderness without technology. Thereafter, Fibbons refused to speak with Johnston and he was removed from the consulting staff and the set.

Gruel was even more determined than ever. He requested a book on the native flora and fauna but was refused. He started to use his 'Ulysses' book for toilet paper when that too was refused him. He drank the water from the nearby postcard-perfect stream and got giardiasis and was sick for another whole episode, holding his hand in front of his face so as not to let the camera see how green he had turned, but the cameraman managed to find an angle anyway since the public had a right to know. After this second illness, Gruel started to look none too good. He was losing weight and had diarrhea and had little potable water and there was really nothing in the area that he knew with certainty to be edible. And the little that he was sure of had been greatly depleted by him over the last thirty days. He felt that he could still survive the remaining thirty days on water alone, basically by going on a hunger strike, if he could find some water that wouldn't make him sick. That became his passion and eventually, in a Eureka! moment worthy of Masterpiece Theatre, he did find an old deserted well a few miles from his campsite. This was the highest rated episode thus far and the world rejoiced at his ingenuity and luck. And Gruel's acting certainly had improved now that it was actually 'real'. But it was also a victory for The Company since they figured that he could never survive on just water for thirty days and since he had now found the water, his primary goal, he probably would give up his search for further food, which might have actually saved him. And since there was an organic farm just three miles further down from the well, which he would certainly have found if he had continued walking and which would easily have sustained him for the remaining time, they were greatly relieved. They started planning the final episodes in which they would have to intervene, deus-ex-machina style, and whisk him off by helicopter to the hospital, saved by the loving arms of technology after all.

So Gruel continued to espouse the benefits of his mush diet and the long-term healthiness of clean living and fresh air, and he sat cross-legged for one entire episode and meditated, and he drank his well water with relish, and he didn't seem to be failing fast enough for The Company. His popularity was higher than Elvis at the height of his pelvis swinging. The Network was thrilled. The Company, however, was worried. They couldn't let him succeed, and they couldn't kill him, mostly because he wouldn't allow access, since much of the crew was now behind him and popular opinion was becoming harder and harder to manipulate.

The only bright spot was the fact that Fibbons looked so terrible. He had lost nearly thirty pounds and was quite drawn and weak-looking. His designer clothes hung on him much to the consternation of the designers, and his hair, well, forget about it, but his sagely beard, though very matted and grey, which made him seem even frailer and older than he was, did engender that guru-like quality he had always been seeking. Often he seemed to be in a trance during a show. If *this* was survival, The Company hoped people were thinking, maybe we really do need the microwave. Do-gooders were trying to find and rescue him and occasionally some hikers would wander onto Ford's property and the National Guard would have to forcibly eject them.

With only ten days to go, Gruel had some kind of on-air breakdown. He was nearly hallucinating by this time, and had long monologues about death and seeing colors and his Oneness with The Universe. The Public was eating it up and transcripts of his ramblings were selling like hotcakes on eBay. But this time, with complete clarity, Fibbons looked straight at the camera, and in a calm, serene, almost Christ-like demeanor, he confessed All to the world: how the show was a scam and he had gone along with it to deceive the viewers because he had been a sinner for the Almighty Dollar and that The Company had tried to poison him and if he died he would have great pride in what he had done here and that all of the listening audience must fight the powers of Corporate Evil at which point he fainted or collapsed or lapsed into a coma or was shot with a tranquilizer gun, no one was quite sure which. He was rushed to the hospital by helicopter with all the trimmings and drama and Grand Music as was promised by The Network. The problem was that the hospital and all its technology couldn't save him. He died there the next day, from 'acute occlusion of the left coronary artery brought on by a high cholesterol and salt diet coupled with malnutrition and exposure.' This was bad for everyone. But mostly, it was bad for Technology (since its infallibility was to have saved him), which was all very bad for IBMMicrohard.

Gruel's funeral was broadcast live throughout the world. The conspiracy theories started immediately as to who had actually killed him, which was never fully resolved, however both The Network and The Company paid large sums to his widow and children. Additionally, a trust was set up in his name by The Company to fund an *Institute for Natural Lifestyles*, which eventually went bankrupt when the Dean absconded with the money to start his own school in Mexico. Gruel became an international hero for standing up to 'The Institution'. IBMMicrohard's competitor created its own show that eulogized Fibbons with reenacted reading from his diaries (which were fortuitously smuggled out from his tent that fateful last night by the cameraman of the *Can Gruel Survive?* show because he had wanted a percentage of the show and had been denied it). Fibbons had been secretly writing the memoirs in his tent at night with a candle he had made from the rancid duck fat, the breathing of which may also have contributed to his untimely death.

His writings were published with Great Fanfare a few months later and the book was hailed as a Masterwork of modern non-fiction, a 'Tome for Our Times' (*New York Times Book Review*). Joe Knowles/Gruel Fibbons Day was created as a new National Holiday. There were parades down main streets in all the small towns, and people from the cities flocked like tourists to get closer to Gruel and Nature. IBMMicrohard went belly-up, and its complicity in Gruel's death was always suspected, but never officially proven. People stopped eating pesticides and hot dogs and Cheese Whiz and Cheetos and Cool Whip and bologna and they began to reverse the exponential obesity epidemic among children. Grubs started showing up on upscale restaurant menus. People quit their jobs (or just lost them since so many had worked at The Company) and moved out to the 'Country' which basically meant fifteen miles further into the suburbs of tomorrow. Organic food became *de rigueur*. Kids stopped believing in the media as being accurate and true, but since adults hadn't believed in it for years, sales of newspapers didn't slump much. The Kennedy assassination files were forced open by the Freedom of Information Act coupled with a violent mob and it turns out that LBJ did it because he was sick of being Vice President and was actually a power-hungry megalomaniac and warmonger. A new era of truth in advertising was ushered in and truth almost was King for a while, but it proved unsustainable due to mass indoctrination.

All The Company Men involved in the *Can Gruel Survive?* project went into a Witness Protection Program funded by The Network. We had all sold The Company stock for pennies and luckily were able to get into The Program since we were all broke and completely disgraced, so we did fear for our lives (and our futures), one way or another.

But at least we're not totally broke and living in some clapboard shack and eating bark and grubs and berries. That would be worse, we all agree, when we get together for Canasta. And we wait for the tide to turn as it always does (remember the sixties followed by the eighties?) and hope we won't be too old to become respected Gurus ourselves one day. Gurus of the Spin Business, the Unsung Heroes of Our Age.

Happy Now?

"I'm not happy," he said. "And I haven't been for a long time." I remember the conversation so clearly, as if it had been recorded directly into my brain, word for painful word.

"It's not just you, it's us, the world, everything. It's, well, you must have seen how disengaged I've been."

"Sure," I said, which was quite plainly true. I had noticed that he was not flourishing. I hadn't been either but I wasn't looking to pack it all up, walk out the door and never look back. I wanted to see where it could go, see a therapist, look at our fears with courage and make some positive changes together. I wanted to treat each other's insecurities with kindness and respect. I just hadn't had the time.

"You don't really love me anyway," he continued. "You just don't want to be alone and you're looking for some nice guy to settle down with."

Now that wasn't fair. I actually loved my time alone, when I had it. But I also wanted to be with him, even when he was moping around which he sometimes did, but I never said he should go.

"I can be alone just fine," I retorted. "But we've put in three years together and I just figured you don't throw that away just because you hit a rough spot. And anyway, I thought I had found a nice guy."

"When was it not rough, where was the spot?" He seemed determined to make me angry. "'Shell,'" he tried his softest voice, "I really think it's over. I think it's done and we just haven't wanted to face it. We don't motivate each other, we don't spark each other's imaginations and make 'the good times roll' together, you know what I mean? We stifle each other, actually. I know it's hard…" At this point he reached over to touch the side of my face, but I leaned away, not wanting to cry. "I don't want to give up either, but I have to, for me. You're a really nice person…"

At this point, I did cry. Copiously. Complete with groans and mutterings and clutching at my stomach to keep from puking on him and hyperventilating to the point of wondering dubiously, then fearfully whether he knew CPR. I had been called a 'nice person' many times in my life during these break-up moments or when someone was looking for a favor, and I was really tired of it. I knew I was 'nice', but I thought this time I had found someone who thought that was a good quality in a girlfriend. He held my hand and brought me a glass of water and kept belaboring his point that he was unhappy. He wanted to fly; he wanted excitement. He didn't want 'nice'. He didn't want to rush into another relationship either, there was no one else in his mind to rush off to, but he felt that we should get used to the idea that one of these days we would run into each other and one of us might not be alone. He had some work on himself he wanted to do, particularly to try to understand why he would stay in a relationship for so long in which he was not happy, and how he could avoid that same stagnation in the future.

He got all of this in without my strongest objections because I was having trouble breathing. He was no flyer. He got carsick. We were comfortable together, he told me so many times. Just the night before we had gone out for what I considered a nice dinner and ran into some friends and had a drink with them afterward. There was no hint, no furtive look, no indication whatsoever of this cruelty to come. We had even had our tarot cards read by a wandering reader in the restaurant and there were no dire predictions. In fact, we analyzed our cards that night in the context of our relationship and how they might be reflected in our future, our future *together*.

"I know this may seem like it's out of nowhere, but I've been thinking about it for a long time." He brought me back to my oversized plaid couch in my small, now claustrophobic living room with a thudding crash. "Actually, last night, when we were talking about what that guy who read our tarot cards said, I just couldn't see my cards in the context of us being together. I could only see how it was for *me*. That was the sign, the final sign that made me make up my mind to tell you tonight, not wait to see what might happen in the future. This is the future. Why pretend anything will change in the future without changing the now?"

"We could go see a therapist," I choked out.

"We should, but not together. I'm sure about this. I'm sure and I'm sorry."

I never thought of Pete as a bad guy. But then he had never shown me this side of himself. He was just sort of down and out, somewhat lost, maybe a little in need of a good shower and a haircut some of the time. He didn't really like his job, whereas I found my job stimulating and even fun sometimes, wasn't sure if he should quit and start his own business, but didn't really have one in mind. He was not self-motivated, that's for sure. But he could be very funny. He could make me feel special. He even made me breakfast in bed a couple of times, with a fresh flower in a little vase and everything. Once, when I hurt my back, he went to the library and got a videotape on deep tissue massage and figured out how to do it. He made me happy, and when he tried, he was a good boyfriend. He was not a jerk. Not this creepy, 'you're a nice but boring person' Pete the Cocksure. Maybe he was just confused, or maybe he changed when I wasn't paying attention. Maybe I cared about him too much to want to notice.

Our relationship had been just fine. We had fun and had even talked about moving in together just a few months before. We met at a party, sort of a fix-up by some mutual friends who had told us about each other in advance so we pretended not to know about the fix-up part and tried to act natural while checking each other out. After that, we had a good first date. We went to a favorite restaurant of mine and had a lot to talk about and we waited a week or so before we had sex and the sex was great, I thought, especially compared to some of the losers I had dated in my recent past.

We found that we had a few friends in common and our friends liked each other and we melded our groups together smoothly. He was kind to my mother and flattered her and she flirted with him in an okay way, and really, it all progressed just fine. Most of the time I really did care about his lack of fulfillment with his job and listened ad nauseam about it, and I shared secrets about myself that I felt I could trust him with. We enjoyed foreign films and rented them about once a week. Generally, this was on Fridays, when I went to his apartment and made him dinner. He liked Chinese food and I like to cook, so I would usually make that on our Movie Fridays. We looked forward to this at the end of the week. Sometimes we wouldn't see each other on Saturday night if we had something else going on, but sometimes we would spend the whole weekend together. Sundays were usually for reading the paper and going out for breakfast and maybe taking a walk in the park near my house. I had a small dog that loved the park and wherever I go he goes, so that was fun and Pete really liked my dog, so that was another good thing.

I knew there were problems. Sometimes we just didn't have that much to say to each other, especially about his job after awhile, and sometimes I wanted to see him more than he wanted to see me. Sometimes he said that he wanted more in his life and I was glad that I was there to be the more for him. Yes, I figured *I* was the more in his life. And that was okay with me since I really had everything I wanted. I liked taking care of him and I liked him the way he was and I figured being content was okay. My parents always fought and I vowed not to have that kind of miserable relationship, so this was really good with Pete. We didn't have even one fight in our few years together, which to me was a good thing. I always thought that was something to aspire to, no harsh words, no anger, just kindness and friendship and occasional good sex. But Pete still wanted more. And so he left and there was nothing I could do about it.

I had to drag myself to work those few weeks after 'the conversation'. I did my job somehow, but I'm sure a banana-motivated monkey could have done it better. One day, a co-worker pointed out that I had worn the same outfit the day before and I honestly hadn't noticed. I ate sandwiches at my desk and said I was saving money if anyone asked me to go out to lunch. Finally, I broke down and told a friend at work and she actually got teary and said she had known something was wrong but didn't want to pry and couldn't believe Pete of all people would be so cold. I felt better telling her and she said that slowly I would forget him and she had someone to introduce me to when I was ready. I sure wasn't ready for that yet, but thanked her anyway and told her I would let her know. At that point, I still hadn't completely given up on Pete, hoping he would miss me and realize that we had had something special after all, something that doesn't come along every day. It was hard buying groceries for only one now and I had little interest in cooking. Chinese food gave me the dry heaves. I went to the library and took out a few books I had been wanting to read and also one called *Wake Up to Your Life* hoping to make some positive changes myself.

A few weeks after this, I heard from a friend that she had seen Pete out on a date with a woman who looked like a prostitute my friend said. She was very dark all over, goth or something and had long fingernails and wore a lot of makeup and did all the talking while they were in the restaurant. My friend said that she was scary looking. And they were at one of *our* restaurants. Well, this information was very hard to take and I had to stay home from work the next day, saying I was sick, which I was.

A few days after that, I had gone with a friend to the local independent theatre that shows a lot of alternative films. We had just sat down when Pete walked right past us holding hands with what must have been this prostitute person. I couldn't breathe as I watched them walk down the aisle. My fingernails dug into my friend's arm and later when I saw the marks I couldn't apologize enough.

She was taller than him and had teased, messy jet black hair and was wearing some kind of teenage throwaway outfit with spike heels. I grabbed my friend and we sneaked out the side door. I cried that whole night in my bed and bought new sheets the next day so that I wouldn't be reminded of him at night too, since those were our sheets together. And it was pretty clear now that we would not be having any more nights together.

Within a few months, as I was trying to get on with my life, I heard of a few more Pete-sightings through friends who felt obligated to share them with me. He had moved into this woman's apartment, someone heard. Someone else heard she was pregnant. A mutual friend asked me out to lunch and told me the shocker. He had married her in Vegas and she *was* pregnant and she was crazy and had gone after him with a knife when he said he wanted to change jobs. She told him he was not leaving her with a kid and no job and he would stay at that job forever if he had to to support them. This friend said Pete looked tired but that he said he was excited about the baby and his new life. He said I would find someone too one day and to say 'hi' for him.

It was my friend who said she was crazy, not Pete. My friend said he had met her once at a dinner party at Pete's apartment to introduce her around and that she broke a plate in the kitchen and screamed at him for burning the steaks. He came out sheepishly and said they should all go out for dinner and they made out at the table at the restaurant and all the friends went home early pissed off that they had to pay for their meals. My friend said he hadn't wanted to tell me before, but felt I could handle it now and besides it just showed that we weren't right for each other and I should feel lucky that it's not me.

But that would never have been me. And it would never have been him with me. This was the way he was with her. And somehow, that made me feel much better.

A year or so later Pete called me to say that he was sorry for the way that he had handled himself during our breakup. He said he had an eight month-old daughter and he and his wife were getting divorced and he still had his same job and would I like to get together for a cup of coffee and meet his daughter. I said yes but didn't show up, which is probably the meanest thing I've ever done.

Are You Insane?

A Quiz

Following is a short quiz. Please answer each question with either a 'Yes' or 'No' answer. Answer each question with the first answer that comes into your mind, do not deliberate as this may skew the results against you. If you feel that you are currently insane, you must still take this quiz for verification.

Your final score will help us determine your sanity/insanity quotient. This score will be kept on file to be released in the event that you commit a criminal offense any time in the future or if we need it for some other purpose. Otherwise, it will only be given out upon request.

1. Do you hear voices in your head?
2. Are you saying you have never heard voices in your head, not even once?

3. Do you judge others to be less than yourself?
4. Do you judge others to be greater than yourself? (You must answer 'Yes' to either (3) or (4)).
5. When you feel insecure, do you blame your parents?
6. When you feel paranoid, do you blame your government?
7. Is there life after death?
8. Do you think you will die tragically?
9. Is your life tragic right now?
10. Do you know the name of the White House Chief of Staff?
11. Do you know whom Drew Barrymore is dating right now?
12. Do you ingest an abundance of mercury or lead?
13. Are you friendly?
14. Are you unfriendly? (You must answer 'Yes' to either (13) or (14)).
15. Do you wash your hands every single time you use the toilet, even if you know where they've been and it's really not necessary?
16. Do you do all you can every day to be a better person? Really?
17. Do you feel that religion is a crock?
18. Do you feel that every other religion besides the one you support is a crock?
19. Are you concerned that the results of this quiz could be misconstrued?
20. Are you thinking of this right now rather than answering the questions?
21. Are you off in your own world most of the time?
22. Is it a better place?
23. If not, do you wonder why you go there at all?
24. If you do not wonder, doesn't that make you wonder about yourself?
25. Do you wonder about yourself often?
26. Is there an equivalent of a cookie to a child once one reaches adulthood? (If you do not understand the question, answer 'No.')

27. Is sex overrated?
28. Or is it just overexposed?
29. If all drugs were legal suddenly, would you shoot up heroin recreationally?
30. Do you think a lot of people would?
31. Is the sky imperceptibly falling inward toward earth?
32. Do you feel oppressed by the smells of the world?
33. Is there an overuse of the color pink in the world?
34. Did you believe in Santa Claus post-puberty?
35. Does a trip to the North Pole seem like a lot of fun?
36. Is the word 'holiday' depressing to you?
37. Are you aware of why we celebrate each specific national holiday?
38. Do you feel that your mind is cluttered by too much useless information?
39. Do you feel that the clutter is creating a lack of space and something has got to give?
40. Do you spend time wondering whether it will be an explosion or an implosion when that time comes?
41. Do you think you would be better off without technology?
42. Do you think you would be better off without trees?
43. Do you think you would be better off without the color mauve?
44. Do you fear yourself?
45. Do you fear spiders?
46. Are you scarier to yourself than spiders?
47. If there is a hell, will you be going?
48. Did you know that only 1/2 of one percent of the people in the United States believe that they will be going to hell?
49. Now, do you believe you will be going to hell?
50. Do you long for the good old days?
51. Would you long for the bad old days, as long as they were old?
52. Do you remember your childhood?
53. Do you remember anyone else's childhood?

54. Do you flinch when someone pretends to slap you?
55. Do you think that this is a natural response?
56. Is there any hope for the world?
57. Do you have a solution for our world's problems?
58. Have you ever thought about it?
59. Do you think of yourself as a visionary?
60. Do you think of yourself as a loser? (You must answer 'Yes' to either (59) or (60)).
61. Do you wonder why you have not yet been recognized?
62. Did you ever want to be famous?
63. Do you think that you are?
64. Is there anyone else in the room here with us?
65. Do you enjoy going to the dentist?
66. Have you ever cried over nothing?
67. Do you love anybody? (Must be a human being, not a pet).
68. Can you feel the earth spinning?
69. Do you ever wonder why we don't fly off?
70. Can you read minds?
71. Do you think anyone can?
72. When you look in the mirror, do you see yourself?
73. In *The Wizard of Oz*, do you think Dorothy was just dreaming?
74. Do you think that Dorothy was crazy?
75. Do you wonder what crazy would feel like?
76. Do you know what crazy would feel like?
77. Have you wondered about your sanity today?
78. Do you have a strong sense that each and every one of us is crazy in our own way?
79. Do you think that if you moved somewhere else that your life would be better?
80. Do you think that no matter where you would go, your life would not be better? (You must answer 'Yes' to either (79) or (80)).
81. When you see clouds in the sky, do you pray for rain?
82. Do you think it would work?

83. Have you ever seen the figure of Jesus in a cloud formation?

84. Was he looking at you?

85. Is there a light at the end of the tunnel?

86. Have you seen it?

87. Do you believe in many things that you have not yourself seen?

88. Do you think that that's normal?

89. If all the people in the world got together and prayed really hard at the same time for something like ending world hunger, would god be more likely to hear and take it seriously, like a protest?

90. Do you secretly hope for the end of the world to end your personal suffering in one big communal bang?

91. Do you have compassion for serial killers?

92. Do you blame their parents?

93. If you answered 'Yes' to #91, now do you think you are going to hell?

94. Do you think that enlightenment is a pipe dream?

95. Do you know anyone whom you consider to be enlightened?

96. If you don't know an actual enlightened individual, doesn't that make you wonder about the validity of enlightenment?

97. Or do you believe that no enlightened person would hang around with you?

98. Do you believe that one human being can truly determine another's sanity?

99. Do you think sanity could be more accurately judged by a computer?

100. Have you heard the phrase 'get a grip' directed at you often in your life?

101. Do you know what 'a grip' is?

102. Do you think that the comic 'Dilbert' is based on real people?

103. Do you think that we would bother to do this test if it had no value whatsoever?

104. Do you consider yourself to be a gullible person?

105. Do you think that these are hard questions?

106. Do you wonder if there is any specific order to these questions?

107. Do you think these questions are stupid and have no bearing on your state of mental health?

108. Do you feel that we have already asked question #98 but stated it slightly differently the other time(s)?

109. If you believe that, do you think we have done this just to trick you? (If you do not believe this, go on to question #114).

110. Have you understood every single question in this quiz?

111. Have you lied on some questions because you thought it would make you seem more sane?

112. Are you concerned about your score on this quiz?

113. Will you share your score with your co-workers?

114. Would you like a cookie now?

Everything's Made in China

I was talking to my friend Tony the other day at the Baja Fresh during our lunch hour break from our jobs at The Gap. We had seniority so we got to take lunch together. Tony reads a lot and watches TV news and those screaming political shows and likes to get into haranguing monologues with me since I don't pay that much attention to what's going on in the world so he can really go off without interruption. Tony feels that these days, everything's made in China. Everything. He thinks it's a big problem. He thinks that one day we're going to care that China has all the money and jobs and then we won't mind paying more for our stuff, but it will be too late. Tony thinks that China is paying its workers way too little and that it's undermining our work force because we see that we can get stuff so cheap that we buy the Chinese stuff instead of our own. He says look at the labels at stores now, things that we used to make, it's all made in China. Target. Staples. The Gap. Banana Republic even. He has worked at The Gap for a while and he remembers when most of the clothes were made in the USA. Not anymore. He thinks that we would make more money per hour at our store if we could charge more for the stuff even though we had to pay more for it. People would just know that it cost that much for that thing, and more money would be trading hands in general. He says it's some kind of trickle down thing, but basically everything is too cheap. He thinks that if we all got used to paying the actual costs, then we would buy less stuff, but we would buy quality and then China would be out of business, even though the quality of the stuff from China has improved lately (there was a time when 'Made in China' meant crap, but that was a while ago). But everybody knows it's still not the same quality American workers produce. When you make more money, you have more incentive to do a good job, at least in this country. He thinks that people are patiently starving themselves in China and saving their money now that all of us are buying their stuff, so that the next generation, or the next one after that (he's not sure how long it's going to take), will take over the world. It's a long-term delayed gratification plan and they're all in on it. He says everything used to be made in Japan and look what happened, they came over here and bought up half of Hawaii and California and think how many more Chinese there are in the world than Japanese. And there's only half of California left. But since it's a global economy now, and since EVERYTHING is made in China, well, it just leads down one road. It's inevitable. We might as well learn Chinese right now, although he's heard it's a really hard language, but we'll be able to quit our Gap jobs and work directly for the Chinese, cut out the middleman, the USA. He said that he looked around his house the other night and just took an inventory of his own stuff. He dared himself to find something made somewhere other than China. It took a while, but he had a Panasonic stereo, Japanese, not Chinese (but it was old, like he said, when Japan was making everything and you wouldn't be caught dead with stuff from China), a Brother fax machine (that's from Malaysia), his Zenith TV was made in Mexico, his V-Tech phone that he was sure was made in the USA since it used to be Lucent, was made in China (and that's another thing, a lot of the brands are stealth Chinese companies, ones that you've always thought of as being from the USA, but they're really made in China, so probably some Americans are involved too and those are the ones that are going to clean up when the Chinese come over here to take over), his General Electric clock radio was made in Indonesia, a Samsung VCR which is Korean (and we really need to keep an eye on them too) and some Ikea furniture, which is from somewhere in the Netherlands or thereabouts. Oh, and his Levis were made in Mexico. He made a special point about that. Not one thing was made in the USA and he drives a Ford, but that's made in Mexico too. And that was it. Everything else was made in China. His drinking glasses, the pots for his plants, the lamps, the stuffed Beanie Baby dog, the candles, the candle holders, the salt and pepper shakers, the scissors, the pet toys, the container that holds the cat food, the shower curtain, the spatula, the wine corker, the pens he writes with, the air conditioner, his shoes, nearly all of his clothes, his computer desk, his serving bowls, every lamp, his bicycle, his toothbrush, the dustpan, the hair dryer (basically everything plastic), the rugs, picture frames, the fan, the blender, the coffeemaker, the curtain rod, his Jensen (another good old American name) TV antennae, the thing that turns a three-pronger into a two-pronger for the electric outlet, fucking everything.

So, eventually we changed the subject and went to Starbucks for latte grandes and I thought that it was all just ranting, like one of those 'everything gives you cancer' statements, but then that night I went home and checked my stuff and he was right.

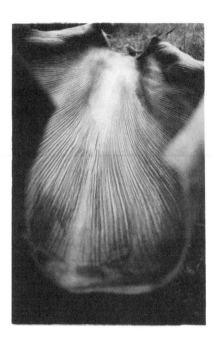

Me Muse, You Artist

I'm a really interesting and attractive person. I have long dark hair and a fair complexion with high cheekbones and a long arched neck and very white teeth. My legs are long and smooth and I have perfect toes, if someone is into that. I have a lovely back with excellent musculature (you may have noticed I work out). I have a college degree in mass communications and I have had several jobs since I graduated which have helped me develop a wide range of skills. I could find a job if I wanted one. The problem is, I don't want one. Well, it's actually not a problem as long as I use my attributes properly. You see, I see myself as a muse.

Someone, preferably a painter or perhaps a photographer, not a musician or a sculptor or a writer, especially not a writer, is waiting to be inspired by me and I figure that's my calling. I'm really not a successful employee. I'd be much better at the higher-level jobs, but I don't want to work my way up some corporate ladder. That's not my style. I don't want to be somewhere at nine am every morning and have my allotted hour where I have my lunch at my desk and scramble out to run a few errands so I can continue my small life. I want to live large, go to grand parties, dress in ball gowns, wear glass shoes and have men drink out of them at the end of the night. I want to be taken care of by someone whom I inspire so that we feel that there is a mutual benefit to our arrangement/relationship. I want to jump from his private plane, spend lost weekends on a secluded beach, swim naked in shark-infested waters when I have my period, I mean really live! And live dangerously! And then have him put it all on canvas or whatever.

So, I put a discreet classified ad in several prominent art magazines which cost me a fortune. It read: "Gorgeous Muse Seeks An Artist To Do Her Justice. You need to be talented and have a promising career. Leave the rest to me… Just call me… Inspiration! Will move to suit, and all the specifics." Anyway, you wouldn't believe all the losers that wrote to me. I expected a few, but this was ridiculous. Maybe they think that I can't recognize a phony when I see one on paper, but I can. A few sent me photos of their art, and since I had a few semesters of Art Appreciation, I was able to separate the good from the bad right away.

So there were two potentials on the short list. I wrote back to them both and sent an especially flattering picture that exposed my best assets and explained that I was the real deal and that they had better take my proposal seriously. I explained my criteria: an expense account; no questions asked about my wardrobe costs; plenty of time set aside for us to just play which is good for the creative process, ideally in four-star locations; monogamy, at least at first, if we find each other attractive; a one-year commitment to be renegotiated annually. In exchange, they get me. All of me, fully devoted, fully servicing their needs and desires while fully influencing their work with all my positive juices, which believe me, are overflowing. I cannot promise that I will release any creative blockages, but I'd be surprised if I didn't (and that's where the yearly revaluation comes in).

Well, one of the potentials didn't like my expectations, but one was still game. He hadn't had a show yet, but his work was acceptable, somewhat abstract unfortunately, but the color choices were innovative. He was forty-seven (rather old, but the monogamy thing is really just to make them see I'm committed to the concept), newly divorced (well, at least he's not married), lives in Florida (another red state, not great, but better than Alabama) and seems to have the means required (although I think he inherited most of it from a rich daddy in the plastics business). We agree to meet halfway in New Orleans (I'm a Texas beauty myself). His name is Julian, which I really like.

I packed all of my best evening wear and casual chic clothing and had my hair and nails done and double-checked the reservation at the hotel he said we were staying at to be sure he wasn't a crook. My tickets arrived by messenger when he said that they would. All seemed legit. I was allowing a bit of excitement to creep into me after I got the tickets. This is what I had prepared myself for, this is what I was born for. I just need a little luck and opportunity (which we all know, you have to make on your own). I read a few uppercrusty magazines and packed them for the plane ride. I called a friend and gave her some minimal information about Julian just in case I ended up in some creepy situation and needed someone to know what I was doing and where I was. You can never be too cautious.

A car met me at the airport with a man in a black uniform holding a card with my name on it, which I thought was a nice touch. He drove me to a lovely hotel near Bourbon Street, old yet tastefully remodeled, just the way I like it. Julian had already checked in and the doorman carried my bags up directly to our room. When the doorman knocked on the door, it opened into a lovely suite with Julian himself, who was not such-a-much, answering. He was shorter than me by several inches, and was balding on the hair parts that were not grey. He was wearing a smoking jacket that looked a little too Hugh Hefner. He smiled broadly, kindly, so that was good, and I tried not to look too disappointed, but I didn't know what to expect since he hadn't sent a photo. It was not about how *he* looked after all, he had said when I asked. The suite was low lit and there were beautiful flowers throughout. He was playing Louis Armstrong and had *The New York Times* open on the couch. He lavishly tipped the doorman and showed me to my room. It was lovely and painted one of my favorite shades of tangerine. Julian said that I looked even better than my photo and that he would give me a few minutes to freshen up and then we should get dressed and go to dinner, as he had reservations at a highly recommended bistro.

He shut my door behind him and I went to the bathroom and looked at myself in the mirror and straightened up my shoulders and thought, maybe he's really talented. I dressed in a skimpy black dress and low heels (I had brought multiple pairs of shoes just in case) and looked fabulous. I decided to put out all the charm I could muster and try to win him over so that the decision would be mine, not his. We did have a delicious dinner. The evening was warm and sumptuous and he was quite smart and we talked about ourselves and what we were looking for in this relationship and our past relationships and all that, which was good to get out in the open right away. His looks were beginning to grow on me, although he was somewhat overweight, with a paunchy belly and not much in the shoulder department. I felt that I could probably take him if it came to that. His skin was awfully pale for a Florida person, but he said that he tried to stay out of the sun for health reasons.

We went to several clubs after that and danced and actually did laugh a few times even though the circumstances were a bit strained, but I was really trying to lighten up the mood and relax him with my charm and sassiness. We walked back to the hotel and he held my hand for the last bit and I let him. I wondered if he was expecting me to sleep with him that night and wondered if it would be good for the deal or not if I did. I decided to wait at least one night. He kissed me lightly, gently, appropriately at my door and said that whenever I awoke we would stroll to breakfast and decide on our day. I liked that and said I had a lovely evening and looked forward to spending tomorrow with him. He smiled.

My bed was comfortable and I slept surprisingly well. I awoke past eleven as we had been out quite late. He was already up and showered and having coffee when I came from the room. I had brought some sexy lingerie and wore it out of the room along with a filmy robe that was revealing but modest. I could see that it worked as he couldn't take his eyes off of me.

We talked lightly for a moment and then he said that he was sure that this arrangement was what he had been searching for in his life and that all he needed was a woman like me to give him inspiration and if I would consent to it, he would like to take me back to my bedroom and show me how he felt about me by consummating our deal. He wanted me to know that he was sincere and could see our relationship spanning many years of great work and personal reward. He would have his lawyer send me the papers as soon as I returned to Texas and we could start making the arrangements for me to move to his villa, which he brought pictures of and would show me over lunch.

What could I say? I was flattered and bowled over by his honesty and no nonsense demeanor. He put his hand on my thigh and I let him and soon we were in the bedroom, bare naked. I knew that this is what I had imagined in a way, but I had hoped he would be a little more attractive and that the whole thing would be less businessy and more romantic. It would certainly have helped me in the muse department. He did his best, and made an effort to make sure I was attended to, but there are some things that either you have or you don't. He did not have much in the way of physical stamina or endowment or general lovemaking machismo. Also, our hips didn't really match so well, but all in all, it went okay, especially for him.

So, we spent the day walking along the streets of the French Quarter and talking and holding hands and looking at the pictures of his estate and dining and dancing and we came back and had sex two more times that night. My flight was the following day. We talked some more about how it would be in Miami, which is where he lived, and how much I would like living there and his family and how I could have whatever I wanted there and he was going to make sure I got it. Also, he said he could feel himself being inspired by my 'musiness,' that's the word he used, and he had several ideas for new pieces, so it was already working. We spent another day together and I was becoming more comfortable with the idea. He was very generous and bought me a gold bracelet at a fine antique shop and he put his hand up my skirt while we had lunch and I pretended that I came, but really couldn't with all those people around and all the pressure.

Anyway, I boarded my plane (his was later that evening) and he kissed me hard at the gate and said he was looking ever so forward to our new life together. I had tears in my eyes as I sat in my seat on the plane and wondered if he could be the one that would change my life. He didn't seem like much of a daredevil and he didn't seem to fully appreciate my many talents, but it was just a long weekend and we would have plenty of time to work it all out later. I had asked him to e-mail me more photos of his paintings and he had said that he would right away and that I should expect to have the papers this week from his lawyer and in the meantime, I should start shopping for my Miami wardrobe and he would send me his credit card.

So I was back home for several days and I checked my e-mail and the mail and nothing. I had expected flowers or a hand-delivered card or *something*. But I didn't really become concerned until the next weekend when I still had not heard from him. I called him at the number that I had reached him at before, and it was disconnected. *Now* I was concerned. I Googled him (if only I had thought of it earlier) and found someone with his name in Indiana. He was a dry goods importer and had been in the news for his policy of giving his workers live turkeys for Thanksgiving and the local PETA chapter had picketed his business. There was a photo and I felt that I was looking at a train wreck, not wanting to know, but unable to look away while the photo loaded. It was him. He had given me his real name and he probably was fairly well-off, but he was no artist and I was no muse.

Personal Expert

How many times have you wished that there was someone in your head, your apartment, your life who was an expert on all things and could answer any question posed to it/him/her? Twenty times a day for me. I never feel totally informed by checking the internet or reading a book or going to the library or asking someone who really should know. I want The Truth. I want it to be definitive. I want to feel that I will not have to ask myself that particular question ever again without being certain that I know the answer. Case Closed.

Instead, most days I feel like the child I used to be asking my parents for answers that they themselves did not know. Sometimes they copped to it and sometimes said ask so and so and sometimes just flat out lied to get me off their backs. But that sense that I had a real answer, something that satisfied and became part of how I saw the world, clearly and without ambiguity, was rarely attained. Mostly it was a half-answer, an appetizer, with the expectation that there would be a main meal *one day*. Sadly, one day really didn't happen too often and you were left with this knowledge hunger, a limbo between knowing enough to speak to uninitiated, disinterested people, to formulate a vague theory or course of action, but not enough to feel confident about it down deep. This is probably how generals feel during a battle when given partial and questionable intelligence and having to make a bold plan knowing the frailty of their reality. No wonder there's so many bad decisions made and so many people feeling generally uninformed and so many ridiculous opinions and so few facts and maybe this is part of the angst in the world, the general malaise, the *grayness* of life. Maybe I'm onto something here.

I just know that if I had the answers to the following questions I would be happier. Period. Happier, more satisfied, less distracted from other thoughts and conversations, more present, more alive and connected. I would be more at peace with the world, less restless, less seeking of otherness to complete me. Basically, having a readily available Expert on any subject that popped into my head would radically change my life for the better.

If anyone has an unqualified answer to the following, please let me know so that I can cross them off my list and get on with my happiness.

1. Is it possible not to be seduced by power? What would be required for this feat? And if it is possible, is it one of those mutations, like someone who is exposed to rabies but doesn't contract the disease?

2. Who says my dog can't learn a language? She knows many words and responds to them and it's not just about the intonation. If I say 'no' with a lilt in my voice, she is quite aware that I'm not saying 'walk' or 'cookie.'

3. Say I lived an alternate life where I ate whatever I wanted and drank a lot of beer and didn't exercise and lay around a lot, and didn't worry too much, basically enjoyed myself more, would I

live longer or less long than my current, careful, moderate but stressful existence that requires constant maintenance?

4. Why is it humane to euthanize a suffering animal but a human cannot legally choose to end his own life humanely when he is suffering?

5. Are soy products good for you or bad for you already? I mean, weren't the Japanese really healthy until they came to America and started eating our crap? I have read that soy alters a woman's hormonal balance (and is this good or bad too?), lowers cholesterol, fights heart disease, is a great meat substitute, prevents cancer and osteoporosis, and also poisons babies in infant formulas, messes with metabolism, and in high levels increases breast cancer and reduces sperm count.

6. Do politicians really believe the things that they are saying? Do they really go to bed at night believing that they are helping this country? Do they honestly see themselves as doing long-term world-building good?

7. Do the fifteen plants I have scattered around my house provide enough fresh oxygen to counter the outside pollution that comes in through the windows? Does it make any dent at all?

8. What's really in our drinking water? And how can the local DWP print regular water quality reports that state that there is no chromium-6 in their samples and then the city is sued for having too much chromium-6 in the water? For that matter, what is in the air? And what about those massive power lines? Are they giving us cancer?

9. How can nails and hair continue to grow after we die? What's fueling the growth?

10. Speaking of hair, how can I lose so many hairs every day and not go bald? I never see little short hairs coming out of my scalp where all the other ones fell out. Explain.

11. Did aliens really land in Roswell, New Mexico in 1947 or any place else at any other time? Are they flying around but choosing not to land? Has anyone actually been abducted by aliens?

12. Is there a Loch Ness monster (Nessie, for the initiated), abominable snowman (Yeti), Bigfoot (Sasquatch—what's with the friendly nicknames?), giant octopus (Leggy?), or any such anomaly alive out there?

13. What are dreams and why do we have them?

14. How did women's orgasms evolve since there is no biological necessity for them?

15. Why do we sleep?

16. Why are we such a miserly people when we have so much? What do we think hoarding will protect us from?

17. Why was John F. Kennedy killed? Who did it?

18. When you burn a candle or lose weight, I know it's transferred energy and water and all that, but what do the wax and the fat really become?

19. Along that same line of thinking, I have heard statistics that hundreds of tons of emissions from vehicles and manufacturing plants go into the atmosphere *every day*. How can that be? Where does it go? Why don't we see it? How is it processed by our environment and our bodies? Why don't we feel the weight in our air? It just doesn't make any sense since that would be millions of tons every year. Why aren't we all dead?

20. If chimps are so close to humans genetically (98-point-something percent related), why don't they speak and have wars and drink wine and since they are five times stronger than man, why don't they rise up and kick our asses?

21. Are we humans on a direct course to create machines that will one day outsmart and kill their makers (think HAL)? If so,

what could induce us to alter our destiny?

22. Is there really a cure for cancer out there or are we just being duped to give money to some massive health care bureaucracy just to make us feel better?

23. What about god? Which religion is closest to the truth or is it all a crock?

24. Do cell phones cause brain damage or does it just seem like it?

25. What makes a huge tree that's been standing for hundreds or thousands of years just fall down one precise moment?

26. What's really living in my carpeting? In my mattress? On my skin? In my stomach? (The answers to these questions may not actually make me happier, but sometimes your imagination is worse than the truth.)

27. Why does looking at, or playing with, a dog or a cat or a stuffed animal even, give one a sense of well-being?

28. Why have human beings evolved to being so fatally flawed? Wouldn't it be better, natural-selection-wise to have us working through our neuroses and violent tendencies and prejudices and hatreds and greed and really bad habits at a faster rate before they do us in?

29. Please settle the nature/nurture debate once and for all. Or at least provide the percentages.

30. Who really was Jesus Christ? Was there any part of a god or spiritual exceptional in him?

31. How is it possible to be in an ever-expanding infinite universe and what exactly is it expanding into?

32. When I drink eight ounces of water, how many ounces actually come out as pee? What happens to the rest of it? And why is pee yellow? Why not the color of what you drank?

33. What happens to the brain during a coma? What makes

someone come out of it after many years?

34. Why is it so hard to see oneself clearly but it's easy to see what's wrong with other people?

35. At what physical point in our lives do we start to deteriorate? What's the physical apex? Is there a mental apex?

36. What percentage of my time in my life is spent on things of no consequence, i.e.: filing papers, worrying, watching dumb TV, talking about things I've already discussed ad nauseam, reading things I'm not even processing, waiting for something to happen, etc.?

37. As an objective observer of my life, does it really have any meaning whatsoever? What can I do to improve in this area?

38. Why do we forget so much of what we've learned, even if it is helpful and we want to remember it? Is there a limited amount of memory space, like in a computer and when you try to add more, it must delete something that isn't used often? Or is there a shelf life for a particular memory, if you don't use it, it gets jettisoned?

39. How can something be of vital importance one day or week or year and then, not much later, not really matter to us at all?

40. If two people really love each other, why isn't that enough to make a relationship work?

41. Do animals have souls? Do we? And what's a soul made up of anyway? And can you sell it? What's it worth nowadays?

42. Did a massive meteor kill the dinosaurs and most other life at the time? Or was it a tiny fungus?

43. What chain of events made human life possible?

44. What's in the center of the earth?

45. Why is it so hard, basically impossible, for man to learn from his mistakes or from the mistakes of history? Why do we

always think *this time* it will be different?

46. Why are creative and funny people so often miserable and moody?

47. Where's the nearest life outside of earth? Do they have anything we could use? Or would they irreparably alter our world for the worse?

48. Why are radical new ideas so vehemently challenged and then years later they are shown to be correct and it seems so backwards and narrow-minded to not have recognized them initially? Why are we so afraid of change? (This goes back to question #45.)

49. How do we psychologically become inured to the pain and suffering of others? Is it some kind of life formula where exposure divided by compassion equals the speed of one's disassociation?

50. Why does Murphy's Law work, even though it's facetious?

51. Is there really such a thing as Karma and if not, why should we do the right thing?

52. Is ignorance really bliss (maybe I've waited too long to ask this one)?

53. Is everything really being made more poorly than years ago or does it just seem like it?

54. Are designer clothes made in the same sweatshops by the same people as those made for Wal-Mart?

55. Is the concept of 'the right thing' universal? Does everyone really know what the right thing is but they choose not to do it? Is this what makes someone a 'bad' person?

56. Along those lines, why is it easier to do the wrong thing than to do the right thing? Is it because often we still feel guilty even if we do what we thought was the right thing? And why don't we do things that we know would be good for us?

57. And finally, if you do the right thing your whole life are you any more likely to feel that your life wasn't a total waste when you're on your deathbed?

58. What's our attraction to mindless 'entertainment'? Reality TV?

59. Do most of the media (TV, radio, newspapers, magazines) assume that the public at-large is educated no higher than the sixth grade level?

60. Why are ants and spiders and those insects that are so much more prolific and industrious and really more creative not running the earth? Why don't they just organize?

61. Why are most rich people even more unhappy than most poor people? And since this is true, why do we all want to be rich?

62. Do most people have kids to give their lives meaning and purpose and usefulness that they fear otherwise they would not find? If so, is this fair to the kids?

63. Is there any truth at all in astrology and psychic phenomena and tarot cards and palm readings and ghost sightings and runes and the Bermuda triangle and the Lost City of Atlantis?

64. If we started today repairing the damage we've done to our environment, would it still be too late to assure human survival?

65. With all that rich food they eat, why don't the French have higher heart disease rates?

66. Why does our eyesight begin to change in our forties almost universally from being near-sighted to far-sighted?

67. If we really care about the education of the children in this country as we purport to, why are our public schools so rigid and structured and authoritarian and overcrowded and under-funded and uncreative?

68. Are most people who home-school their kids especially religious or antisocial?

69. What is biologically or physiologically involved in a chemical attraction between two people?

70. Why do some things, like blue cheese, smell terrible but taste delicious? Why did the first people try them?

71. Is there any truth at all to people being 'turned gay' by society, like people are turned mean or turned to Christ?

72. How could all dogs on this planet have come from wolves, I mean, poodles and chihuahuas and shih tzus and yorkies? What if someone had been cross-breeding us?

73. Why don't we or can't we utilize more of our brains to solve all these personal and world problems? And what could be accomplished if we were able to utilize 100%?

74. Why is math the only discipline that will provide only one correct answer?

75. How can fungi live underground for tens of years and not die out? What are they living on?

76. How can ants fall from thousands of times their body height and not be smashed by the ground?

77. Why does change happen so incrementally if Darwin's theory of mutation is true?

78. Why do we tend to want to feel sorry for ourselves?

79. What happens to the brain when one meditates properly?

80. Why do some people have so much better memories than others? Are they just paying more attention?

81. Why does camouflage look so goofy up close but really blend in far away?

82. Is it just an urban myth that scientologists believe that L. Ron Hubbard was taught by aliens and that's what they find out

when they give their life savings and reach the highest levels within the organization? (If not, this just saved some people a lot of time and money).

83. How many modern inventions originated with or are based on the wheel?

84. Through grief or insanity or a terrible crisis, is a human being capable of literally killing himself through his own mind? Can we break our own hearts?

85. What are the odds of being born a genius? Will we one day genetically alter fetuses to breed geniuses? What percentage of geniuses never amount to much or at least never live up to their potential? Why? And what did we learn from studying Einstein's brain after his death?

86. How can we be so weak and so powerful at the same time? So smart and yet so stupid?

87. Why do mosquitoes and flies bite some people but not others?

88. If we all moved to Mars, how would we feel about Earth? Would it feel like when you move from your hometown?

89. Why are people in the southern United States so conservative when they have all the warm weather and great beaches and good vacation spots?

90. And what would the United States be like today if the South had won the Civil War? And if some states still want to secede, why not let them?

91. Why are hemp and pot illegal really? You can't overdose on pot no matter how hard you try, it's better for you than drinking and smoking, it has medicinal applications, it isn't the 'gateway drug' (alcohol is), and hemp has an enormous economic potential in everything from food to fiber to oil for fueling cars. Is it the pulp-paper-from-trees-industry lobby, or is it that we want to keep the prison economy going or is it

that the government is afraid that we'll all start enjoying our lives and stop working to buy their crap?

92. If everyone on earth had to take one hit of acid once for some kind of collective mind-expanding test, would there be any lasting sociological or biological harm? What about the benefits?

93. If you lie once or twice, does it become progressively easier? If so, is this because we lose respect for ourselves?

94. Are major corporations the root of most social evils?

95. If we took the money out of politics, would it really get any better?

96. Is being a cynic just a form of laziness?

97. Whose big idea was it to feed ground up parts of cattle to cattle? Or to force-feed them corn for that matter, when they naturally eat grass? Why don't we ban these practices?

98. And why do so few humans understand that what you put into your body *becomes* your body?

99. Can anything survive a nuclear holocaust? How soon until we find out?

100. What can an individual do to end world hunger and poverty?

101. Why do cats and dogs sleep so much? Are they just bored with their lack of options?

102. When our government knew highjacking planes and crashing them into buildings (even just highjacking planes in general) was a possibility, why didn't they insist on locking, reinforced cockpit doors years ago? Or even the insurance companies for that matter. Wasn't anyone awake?

103. Why aren't we given more life preparatory classes in high school and college? Is it too hard to find qualified teachers?

104. How are governments able to keep their conspiracies under wraps for years and years? Are the conspirators threatened with torture or death if they squeal? And do most of those complicit in the crimes confess on their deathbeds, hoping for redemption, but we just never find out?

105. How could someone with George Bush's qualifications and experience become president of the United States? Has he opened the door so that literally anyone can be president? Could that somehow be a good thing?

106. Is there so much suffering in the world because human beings are just not enlightened? And why do our ethics and maturity lag so far behind our intelligence and ingenuity?

107. Why does life have to be an incurable disease? Will there one day be a cure for death? And then what?

108. Is there any form of life after death whatsoever? And will we ever have any further contact with those who have died?

109. When people see white lights and hear voices and feel drawn toward something beautiful and compelling during near-death experiences, is this just mass hypnosis from all the press and the desire for it to be true? Will anyone ever really come back from having died and give us the definitive proof of an afterlife?

110. And say we could live to be 200, would we just keep getting smarter and smarter? Or just really bored and depressed about how the world was going?

111. Why is so much destruction and depravity and discrimination and atrocity committed by so-called religious people? Aren't they ashamed of themselves? Do they think they will still get into heaven?

112. Why didn't somebody kill Hitler early on?

113. Did we really think we were doing the right thing when we dropped the bombs on Japan? Or was it done purely in self-

interest?

114. Why do all the pictures of aliens by abductees look the same? Is it the same gang of hooligans every time?

115. Does the concept of destiny hold water?

116. Can people really move objects and bend spoons with their minds? And if so, why don't they try to expand their repertoire?

117. Should we keep experimenting with cloning and stem cell research and nanotechnology and smart computers or is this all a pandora's box?

118. How could human beings actually kill every last passenger pigeon in this country when there were more of them than all birds on earth combined when Europeans first arrived in the United States? How could we have been so short-sighted? And how does this parallel what we are doing to the earth now?

119. Why is animal experimentation legal when human experimentation is considered immoral? Especially since there are humans willing to submit to experiments but we cannot derive consent from animals.

120. Do we teach our children aggression or is it a natural, innate, instinctual response to our lives?

121. Along the same lines, is stress simply the proper response to our fears?

122. And why are we all so motivated by fear?

123. Why are breasts sexy to humans but not to other mammals (as far as we know)?

124. Approximately when can believers expect the second coming or the rapture since they seem to be getting anxious?

125. When is the next ice age coming? Will there be any place to go on vacation?

126. Why do so few people choose to live an aware, conscious life? If this is the only crack we may have at a life, shouldn't we live it fully? Are we just kept too busy with life's maintenance to digest this? Or do most people believe that they will have other chances?

127. Is anybody really watching what we do (some may call this possible entity the 'universal observer')? And if there is an 'observer', does that influence outcome?

128. Along those lines, will quantum mechanics actually prove that there is uncertainty behind all atomic interaction? If so, how could we utilize this knowledge to create positive change?

129. Why do so many seemingly 'normal' people find themselves drawn to and supporting fanatical, even crazy whack jobs like Jim Jones or David Koresh or Adolph Hitler or Pat Robertson?

130. Was there really an 'Eve', a woman from whom we are all descended?

131. Why do we sometimes have a visceral negative reaction to someone we don't even know?

132. Has anyone ever really had a past life, whether as a human or a goat or snake or Cleopatra?

133. Do rude people care somewhere, deep down, what others think of them?

134. Why do most people have a deep need to feel superior to someone else? And is bigotry simply inherited ignorance?

135. Why is there so much gun violence in the United States, especially when compared with other countries? What can we do about it?

136. What are we supposed to be doing here exactly? Just to become the best person you can be seems like a short-sighted goal.

137. Why are there so few truly heroic figures in the world? So few exceptional human specimens like Abraham Lincoln or Martin Luther King or Gandhi or Eleanor Roosevelt? And so many George Bushes.

138. In that vein, where does courage come from?

139. Why, in the twenty-first century does anyone care what other adults do in the privacy of their own bedrooms (or any other room in their house for that matter) as long as no one is being hurt?

140. And why are we such puritans about sex in this country and yet we use sex and half-naked women and men and children to sell just about anything, any time to anybody?

141. On that note, why isn't hypocrisy illegal and punishable by hard time?

142. Who actually wrote the Bible excerpts? (And who chose what was included in it and why?) The Dead Sea scrolls? And who was Shakespeare?

143. Is war ever the right course of action?

144. Can parrots understand the context of anything they are saying? Can dolphins understand human communication? Can any human understand them?

145. Why do people in this century still insist on uninformed, embarrassing ideas like there is no evolution nor global warming nor oil shortage or animals don't feel pain or the possibility of life outside of earth is unlikely or the Grand Canyon was created in 'the big flood'? How do we non-violently knock them upside the head?

146. How can someone purposely commit a horrible atrocity against another and go on to live with seeming self-immunity?

147. Is there a sanity threshold in the average person, in which, when pushed past it, any person could become a sociopath, capable of just about anything?

148. Is there such a thing as bad luck? Can someone actually be lucky or unlucky?

149. What is it in human beings that makes us search for things we don't understand and try to make sense of them? Is our search for order commendable or merely full of hubris? Do any other animals have this desire? Will it be our demise?

150. Will I ever really know the answer to any of these questions? And if not, why do I allow them to concern me, since they function only to make me feel unfulfilled? And is this searching ultimately what it means to be human?

You

You wake up in the middle of the night, hungry and needing to pee. You don't get up since it will fully wake you and you know that you shouldn't eat in the middle of the night anyway. You try to think of blank nothingness so that you can fall asleep again. You have a vague realization that blank nothingness is very hard to achieve and make a note to think on this later even though you know that you will completely forget all about it even as you remind yourself now to remember. If somehow you do remember to remind yourself, you will rack your brain for a few minutes seeking this interesting yet fleeting thought, in there somewhere, ripe to be plucked and expressed if you just had a better retrieval method, and finally you give up. Deep down, you know this is a little trick you do to yourself in these moments of discovery to make believe that your life is more in control than it really is; you do not even consider getting up to write it down because you have already convinced yourself that you will surely remember it since it is so compelling. You try to stop thinking about all this since you have to be up early for work and you don't want to be tired all day and you know how you get. You know this pressure makes it harder to fall asleep but you can't really stop doing it to yourself. You do not look at the alarm clock to see what time it is since this is a sure way to ratchet up the pressure. You count to one hundred slowly with the words 'one thousand' in between the ones and twos, hoping the monotony of the language will lull you back to that land to which you want to return. You were actually having an interesting dream and hope somehow to will yourself back into it to see what happens. Eventually you are successful, falling asleep anyway, but you don't remember if you dream.

You wake in the morning, tired despite your best efforts to get to bed on time and stupefy/numb yourself back to sleep in the middle of the night. You are on a diet and not eating much, and know this could well awaken you with hunger pains, which it does regularly, although last night's insomnia you think was just stress-related, even though you were hungry. You go into the bathroom and use the toilet, feeling good to get yesterday out of you, since it was nothing special. You go into the kitchen and make yourself a cup of hot, steaming coffee with nearly a third milk, just the way you like it and expect it to be every morning. You sip it slowly, reading whatever piece of written material is left on the kitchen table from yesterday's mail or a new magazine or some section of the newspaper you hadn't yet gotten to. Sometimes, when you are really tired, you read something you have already read since that's what is in front of you. You're aware of this as you are doing it, but think to yourself that maybe you missed something last time you read it since you were really tired.

You pet your cat and put out some food for him since once again, you will be at your job for his entire day. You lay out an outfit on your bed, except for the shirt that you are hoping the shower steam will unwrinkle. You step into the shower, convinced it will revive the rest of you that the coffee didn't reach. You let the water run down your face, really feeling its pressure and heat. It feels especially good to you this morning. You realize that you have now wet your hair and this wasn't supposed to be a wash-your-hair-day, but it is too late now so you soap it up. You shave your armpits since you will be wearing a sleeveless shirt under your sweater and in case you take off the sweater in the course of the day, you want to appear groomed since you do interface with the general public and this is specifically noted in your contract with your employer. In fact, you think grooming may have its own paragraph.

You dry your hair. You realize that you did not factor this added time into your morning because you were not going to wash your hair, so you have to pick up the pace a bit. You look in the freezer and find a frozen entrée for lunch and take a muffin out of a box on the counter and say goodbye to the cat and leave, planning to eat the muffin en route. This is not how you like to start your morning, rushing off. You like to eat the muffin or piece of toast or bowl of cereal at home and contemplate the ride to work or what CD you'll listen to or what calls you will have to make once you get to work. But you also realize that you can't have everything the way you want it. In fact, you can't have much at all the way you want it and you've gotten pretty used to that.

You drive to work in the traffic of others like yourself. You all have to be somewhere at roughly the same time which you think is rather inefficient. You listen to Neil Young sing about a small town and you wonder if you would be happier there. You think you might be happier in some ways and not in others. You wonder how you would make a living in a small town. You wonder if making a living is so important after all. You wonder if you would meet interesting people in a small town. You wonder why you wonder that since interesting people must be everywhere. You figure you need to save some money in order to move anyway so you shouldn't waste your time wondering about a different life that you can't afford. You wonder why it all comes down to money eventually. You wonder if you should try to get a better job that pays more so you could speed up the process of getting on with the rest of your life which you assume will be better. You wonder if you can truly be living in the here and now if you feel this way. You wonder when you look back on your life if it will add up to something. You decide to think of something else since you are getting depressed and you have a long day ahead of yourself and you are expected to be cheerful at work. In fact, this is also in the contract. You wonder if signing that contract made you more aware of being cheerful and pleasant or if you would have been anyway. You figure that you will never know since it was mandatory and you can't see the same coin from both sides at once.

You pull into the underground parking lot at the office complex where you work and park your car in the space with your number on it. You know that some people in your office had an argument over who would park where and you feel you got a pretty good space out of it. Your space is close to the elevator and on an upper level so you don't have to go round and round and get dizzy getting down to your space. You know that this is all just kidding yourself to feel better about coming into work, about feeling that you are special somehow, that someone cared about your feelings and wanted you to know that they were taking your concerns to heart when they made out the parking grid instead of actually giving you a raise.

You look at your co-worker's car parked next to yours and yours seems shabbier somehow and it needs to be washed and it is a less expensive model than your co-worker's and you wonder if your co-worker makes more money than you or if his priorities are just different and he doesn't eat out much or buy stuff for his apartment. You have a vague sense that this is why you come to work, so that you can own things that in turn seem to own you, and this makes you uneasy, but you don't know what the alternative is. You see everyone else doing the same things, wanting the same things, and no one is offering any other viable kind of model so you figure that basically, this is the life paradigm. You know that you don't fully buy this but you really don't have time to delve into this now because the elevator is here and you have to get into your cheery mindset, which might take a few minutes. You make a mental note to think about it more deeply later, when you have some quality time, secretly hoping that this isn't another memory trick you do to yourself to recall those half-awake epiphanies, but you think it might be, and you still don't write it down.

It's Cold Outside

I once knew this guy in Chicago named Finn. He was a friend of a friend of mine, so I didn't know him that well. Truthfully, I feel that I know him now, now that I don't know him at all, better than I knew him then when I would see him around once in a while. This is because I have thought a lot about him since then and in those days I didn't think much of him at all. I was doing pretty well then, had a good job downtown, went down to Rush Street and had quite a few drinking buddies and never had trouble finding a date, and to me, Finn was kind of strange. He didn't seem to be part of any group of friends; never even mentioned girls. He did temp work or something like that and took classes at the Art Institute when he had the money. He dressed really weird, in striped bell bottoms and ripped t-shirts, combat boots, stuff like that that you know he bought for a buck at a thrift store in a bad neighborhood. In those days especially I noticed things like that because I spent a lot of money on my clothes.

I met him at a party at my friend Steve's house, I don't know, at least fifteen years ago, when I was living that life. Steve lived in Wrigleyville in an old greystone that he had lived in for over five years and had a whole floor to himself. It was a three bedroom apartment with great bay windows and hardwood floors that he paid like five hundred a month for because he had lived there for so long and we were all envious because we just recently had the money to afford a decent place but rents weren't cheap like that anymore. So anyway, he had a few parties over there and we all pretty much knew each other, except Finn who didn't know anyone but Steve. Steve had taken a few art classes at one point and that's where they had met. Steve had always told me what an interesting guy this Finn was and that he was really smart and talented and that he had a lot of things figured out, but he had a hard time with girls and was kind of a loner. So, I went over to talk to him for the first time that night.

Again he was dressed all wrong in lime green polyester pants and a bowling shirt with the name 'Bud' on it. I saw that he didn't have a beer so I brought him one. He nodded, but didn't say thank you or anything, and took a drink. He gave off a weird vibe, distant and curious at the same time. I said that I had heard about him from Steve and that Steve thought he was doing some good work at the Institute.

"Work?" He said. "I wouldn't call doing what you love work. Work is what I get paid to do."

I asked him what he would call it. "Pain," he said after a thoughtful pause.

"So, I should say that Steve said you're doing some good pain at the Institute?" I asked, laughing to myself at my quip.

He looked me over. I was wearing a snappy outfit and new shoes. "No, *you* should call it work," he said.

"So, you love pain?" I asked, trying to understand and not get pissed off at his attitude, but I was already set off by his not thanking me for bringing the beer.

"From my pain things come out of me that I can embrace and love. If I don't feel anything, I can't create anything meaningful.

And since most of my life has been sort of painful, to answer your question, in a way, yes." He took a drink of his beer and looked down at his shoes.

"Yeah, my life's been sort of painful too, except it's getting better lately," I said vaguely.

He looked at me again, right in the eyes, not the way most people look at you. I would have walked away from him, but for the moment I was interested, and I figured I wouldn't have a conversation like this for the rest of the night, that's for sure. I got the impression he didn't see much pain in my eyes, because he didn't say anything.

Then he asked, quite sarcastically I thought, "So, what do you *do?*"

I could tell he didn't really care and had already made up his mind what kind of work someone like me would do and what kind of person I was, so I said, "I work with handicapped kids" which wasn't true at all. His eyes brightened a bit. I kept on, "Yeah, I try to teach them to stand and walk and use their wheelchairs, that sort of thing. It's very rewarding."

He looked in my eyes again. "Isn't your name Brad?" He asked.

"Yeah," I said.

"Actually, you're a bond trader down at the board of trade," he said. I swear I blushed.

He nodded and walked away. I think he left shortly after that.

How fucking odd, I thought, yet I didn't immediately forget that conversation and I have long since forgotten all the rest of the conversations that night and subsequently many other nights I have forgotten not only the conversations, but the nights as well.

I could see why the guy had problems with girls. At that time in my life, this is what I knew about women: they are attracted to money and fast cars and things you give them and great meals and nice clothes and confidence; they want to know that you have potential, even though you know that most of these relationships are going nowhere and any potential you may have they will never get to realize, but in the here and now, you show them a good time and they put out and everybody's happy. So, this guy Finn had no chance.

Maybe he had some art talent, maybe not, but that was such a tough business and it was years before you made anything, if ever, and no woman worth anything would wait that long. You could tell he was his own best friend in every sense of the word.

So, that was maybe June, I remember because it was already hot. I didn't see Finn again until I was over at Steve's watching a ball game at Wrigley Field from his rooftop deck and Finn stopped by. It was maybe September now and still hot and we were drinking and sitting under an umbrella and kind of lazy-afternoon drunk by the time Finn showed up. His hair was all messed up like he just woke up and he looked his usual wacky self. He nodded to me and waved to Steve and basically ignored the other two guys up there. Steve asked him about some art piece he was working on and Steve seemed impressed by the sheer size of it and we went back to watching the game.

Later I asked Steve something about covering up the deck when it snows and then Steve said to me, but including Finn, "So, Finn is going to go without a coat this winter. He's been working on mind over matter, bending spoons and shit like that to strengthen his mind in a way so that he can control his senses. He figures he can transcend Chicago's winter." Finn looked uncomfortable that Steve had told me, like I wouldn't get it and that I shouldn't be included in things that were way beyond me. I nodded, not sure what to say.

"You really think you can do it?" I asked finally to break the awkward silence.

"Yeah, I've been preparing for a long time. I gave away my coat, just to be sure."

"So, what kind of mental training have you done?" I wanted to know.

"It's using parts of your brain that you normally wouldn't. You do exercises, slow your heartbeat, I can't explain it. You just have to believe that you can do it."

"If anyone can do it, it's Finn. He's nuts and will never say die," Steve adds. "He'll do it."

"But you could just wear a bunch of layers and wouldn't need a coat," I just realized.

"No layers. One shirt, one sweater, one pair of pants, underwear, socks, shoes. No scarf, no hat, no gloves. Feel the cold, but not let the mind interpret it as being something it can't deal with." I could tell he was preparing himself as he spoke.

"I've lived here my whole life and have never gotten used to the cold," he continued. "I figured it was just mental laziness and human beings can get used to anything. People lived through the Holocaust, they survive in Alaska and Northern Canada and Iceland, they live in the Sahara Desert, I can go without a winter coat. It's really no big deal."

It was to me since I also hated the cold and in the back of my mind was waiting to make enough money to get a place in Florida or Arizona for the winters. I had just bought a shearling winter coat and I remember thinking I would never do something so stupid as to freeze to make a point. I guess his look at me was justified, because I didn't get it. Then.

My interest in Finn grew a little after this and I kept up with him from time to time through Steve. I think it was November the next time I asked him how it was going with no coat. By this time of year, it's definitely cold and I had been wearing my shearling for over a month now. Steve said he was doing great and believed that it really was no big deal for him. He would start to get cold and then he would meditate for a minute and it would just go away. It was worse for Finn because he didn't have a car and he didn't have that many friends or a girlfriend to give him rides, so he was taking the el train a lot and that was the worst, standing up on that platform in the wind. I got cold thinking about it. I admitted to Steve that I was weak and undisciplined and was okay with that and we laughed and agreed that we couldn't do it.

Around Christmas I was doing some shopping downtown after work and I was waiting for my car at a lot and Finn walked by on the sidewalk. He was true to his word and was wearing only a collared shirt under a crew neck sweater. He looked damn cold to me and there was some snow or frost on his eyelashes.

I offered to give him a ride and he thought about it for a second and then said, "No thanks, I need the exercise." We stood there and I asked if he was sure.

"Always," he said and smiled and walked away.

I watched him walk down the street and get mixed up in the crowd and I knew that he was strange and, for good or bad, also knew that I probably wouldn't know too many people like him in my life.

So I got busy at work and pretty much forgot about Finn except once in a while when I would mention him to a date for laughs or over lunch with some friends when they mentioned how freakin' cold it was outside. Now February is the coldest, dirtiest, grayest, longest damn month in Chicago. By that time, you are so sick of the weather and the clouds and you start to notice that everywhere else in the country there are signs of spring but not in your neighborhood and this is when even Chicagoans get fed up. I went to another party at Steve's and was about to leave and realized that I hadn't seen Finn or caught up on his adventure. I needed the newest installment to share at work. Steve shook his head, his disappointment apparent when I asked.

"He didn't make it, man. He stuck it out til the end of January, but he just couldn't take another month or more. He was freezing all the time by the end. He wasn't using the heat at his apartment so that he could stay acclimated and it was killing him. It was just too much and his meditation wouldn't work under those conditions. He called me, really pissed at himself when he finally turned on the heat. What could I say? I said it was okay and he had made it that far, and that was a victory, but he was really worried how it would affect his art, since he saw it as weakness and just plain taking a short cut and he could forget about any creative breakthrough or mental strength. I think he's embarrassed after talking about it to be seen outside with his coat on. You gotta admire the guy for trying though."

I left the party sort of depressed. I wanted him to make it, I realized. I liked that he was out there, doing something heroic in a way; that he existed. I liked that I knew him and could mention that he was doing this crazy thing once in a while. It made me more interesting to *me*. I didn't turn on the heat in the car on the way home in sympathy and enjoyed the cold like a slap in the face when you know you need it, and something subtly changed in me after that.

I started to notice about myself that I was someone who didn't like to be hungry or thirsty or too hot or too cold or uncomfortable in any way. I started to see people that I normally would think of as dweeby or strange and to try to figure out what their story was. I started to be more tolerant and more forgiving and I let people cut into my lane when I was driving and I saw outlandish clothes as just personal taste and guys with dangly earrings weren't necessarily gay and I even dated some smart girls who weren't that cute. I would let myself sweat sometimes and not turn on the air conditioning and I was more aware of my body turning fleshy and flabby and soft when it happened and I had the feeling that that's what my mind looked like inside. I realized that I wasn't a Finn and I was never going to fight in a war and I would probably not have survived the holocaust and that when it's cold outside I dress appropriately and I don't push myself the way some others might, but I did develop a strong interest in art.

And I realized that I was never going to be extraordinary and I was much more ordinary than I had ever suspected. I tell myself that having this knowledge is better than living with a comfortable lie, and then I try to believe it.

I ended up staying in Chicago and got married and moved to the suburbs and had two kids and we never did get that place in Florida. In my life I never took any real chances, but meeting Finn changed me and if I had never known him I would not be the man I am now. That man would be any one of my friends. And in an odd way I resent it because it planted a small kernel of doubt in most everything I do and made me in some way question things I would have accepted wholeheartedly before. It has made me neither solid nor adventurous, neither creative nor secure, neither friendless nor gregarious, neither deeply committed nor disinterested, neither satisfied nor truly wanting, neither fully here nor there.

Bath Toys Are Pack Animals

Along the rim of the bathtub in the home of a young family in an American suburb of a large metropolis lives a pack of wild bath toys. They were thrown together and became a clan whether they liked it or not when the parents bought the bath toys willy-nilly for their young son. They had no choice in the matter of where they would live, and have tried to make the best of it. Rubber babies coexist with a plastic flying saucer who has a friend that is a shocking pink pig. They consider themselves free range toys since they maintain their own thoughts and ideas and do whatever they want when the family isn't looking. Mostly they argue. When the family is paying attention they are quiet and play nice together. They only behave themselves because they realize that they could be tossed in the recycle bin if anyone were to find out what was really going on.

The pack consists of: three pink or flesh-colored rubber babies of varying sizes; Wee, the smallest stands with arms outstretched as if wanting to be hugged, which is basically true, Falls lies on her stomach with her arms straight forward, supporting herself, seemingly uncomfortably, and Tall Paul, the largest of the babies, reclines on his back with his hands clasped behind his back and his eyes closed, apparently relaxed or even sleeping but in actuality keenly aware of and able to see everything; Piggy, the aforementioned shocking pink pig; Bluey, the obligatory rubber duck, except he's blue like the color of the sky, which is impossible in nature but not in toy makers' imaginations; Zap, the neon green glow-in-the-dark flying saucer, which was purchased on a whim, and finally; the letters 'C' and 'Z', these being orange and red respectively and rather small compared to the rest of the toys. 'C' and 'Z' are regularly picked on for being letters not animals and for whatever reason one of the others might think of.

There is a hierarchy among the toys. Sadly this is true in most packs as one is the alpha and one is the beta and everyone else has their days in the sun and many more in a dark closet. Tall Paul considers himself the alpha toy. He bosses the others around and lords it over them in every possible way. He's the biggest, he's human-shaped (and they are all aware that humans dominate in the outside world), and he was one of the first toys in the tub so he feels entitled. However, the favorite toy of the child of the family is Wee. This really irks Tall Paul. Tall Paul feels that if he could just be the favorite toy as well as the leader, he could be King.

But the child prefers the cuteness and open arms of the naked Wee to the smirking and conniving Tall Paul and no one can blame him. So even though Wee is quite small and seemingly helpless among the pack, his position is quite strong since he's the child's favorite. Because of this, the other toys treat Wee well and want to be around him.

Falls is basically second-in-command and the others go down in authority somewhere from there. Piggy is not taken very seriously since she is a pig and short and squat and has a rather blank expression and doesn't get involved much with the others one way or another. She's not aloof exactly, just … mature.

Bluey is continually harassed because rubber ducks were the original bath toys a long, long time ago so he is considered old fashioned, but he is also teased because of his rather odd coloring which seems to make no sense. He defends his blueness by saying that the sky is where ducks live most of the time and he probably just got too close to it and it rubbed off, but no one accepts that explanation, even though it would bring him up a peg or two if it were true.

The flying saucer Zap, being neither animal nor vegetable is treated rather poorly. He is called not-of-this-earth and compared to an abominable snowman or the Loch Ness monster. He is basically ignored by the child as well, since Zap is at his best in the evening at which time he actually does glow a quite nice fluorescent green, unfortunately the child is asleep, not bathing.

The letters are just way down the ladder even from Zap since they are not even based on things. They are based on the alphabet which doesn't really count for much in this group. And 'Z' doesn't even speak so 'C' has to do all the defending of words and the representing of all letters which gets rather tiring so 'C' oftentimes just takes the abuse rather than get all worked up over the illiterate bunch's rot.

It may look like these bath toys are not communicating in any real way, but that assumption would be incorrect. They cannot move, which is very frustrating to them as you can imagine, but they have a quiet encoded language that is intelligible to them alone. They are also able to communicate when they are squeezed; that squeak that emanates is heard soundly by all and demands attention. A lot of meaning can be conveyed by just one squeak.

They love the bath time because they get to float around which feels to them almost like mobility, as if they are swimming on their own. They suck water in through their holes and can squirt it out at each other. This is a very fun game. They also like to be touched and fondled, so this time is very special indeed. The toy that receives the most attention by the child during bath time is looked up to for the rest of the day. They even smile, although after awhile the effort hurts so they have to stop, but they often continue smiling on the inside.

Today, bath time has recently ended and all the toys are wet and happy. They floated along with the currents and banged into each other like bumper cars and were stroked and squeezed and all went well. However, Tall Paul is angry that Wee, once again, received the most attention from the child. He is trying to devise a strategy to divert this attention from Wee onto himself. Zap and Tall Paul and 'C' and Falls are in a pile in the corner of the tub. "What if we hid Wee so that they only had us to play with?" Tall Paul wonders.

"How absurd," says Zap, "Really, how hard would he be to find?"

"I could make it tough. I could, well, I could sit on him."

"At least you were noticed. The child is much too young for letters or to have any understanding of language. I have years to wait and then perhaps he will not bathe in the tub as the old ones don't. I may never be played with at all, and I've heard that there are toys that actually are allowed to *sleep* with the boy." 'C' sometimes becomes inconsolable like this.

"Stop your bellyaching," asserts Tall Paul. "All of us would get more touch time without that begging Wee. Look at him, always looking for a hug."

They look over to the other rim. Wee has his arms outstretched as usual. "Disgusting," Falls agrees. "So desperate."

Zap chimes in: "You think you have it hard, being a letter or being passed over now and then. What if you had a truly remarkable talent that went forever unnoticed. I glow! Can any of the rest of you say that? I will never get my proper due!"

"Your proper due?! I am forever ridiculed for being passé and am disregarded. 'Can't they think of anything new, I mean, really, a rubber duckie?' But I am new! I am blue! I have feelings too!"

"Keep it down, clown!" Tall Paul rudely rhymes. "You're like a Lincoln log or a choo choo train. Used up and old news. You're about as old as taking a bath itself. Nobody—"

"Don't any of the rest of you get tired of this same old tirade?"

This voice comes from all the way down the tub, from Piggy. "I certainly would like some peace and silence so that I can think of larger global concerns. Let's show each other some respect and keep quiet if none of us has anything nice to say."

"What a bore!" says Tall Paul.

"At least we're social," pipes in Falls.

Wee just keeps smiling his small Mona Lisa smile in the opposite corner of the tub where he and 'Z' were left after the bath. 'Z' is very happy to be near Wee. His status has gone up by this proximity. Even though it's just happenstance where the child places them after the bath, these things count among the pack.

At that moment, something horrific happens. The family dog, a brutish black hairy beast comes into the bathroom and, after sniffing around a bit, carries off Wee in its pink and drooling mouth. He squeezes Wee mercilessly as he goes, teasing them all with his offhand power.

'Z' who never says a word, screams. 'C' faints. Zap turns his head away in fear and tries to make himself small.

Tall Paul chuckles. "That'll teach him," he muses. "He'll come back all chewed up and not very desirable for play time."

"You horrible bully!" 'C' has woken up.

"Let's all hope that there is no damage from this vicious attack," Piggy intones from the sidelines. "I believe we can all relate to the horror Wee must be feeling."

Falls smirks. Tall Paul interjects. "Maybe he likes it. He's an attention hog after all, no offense meant to the other hog here, and maybe being gummed feels good to him." Falls giggles, participating in the cruelty.

"You will get your comeuppance, young man," Piggy says seriously and turns her head to the wall, signifying she is done listening to this rubbish.

"Are you praying to the toilet god for the safe return of the runt?" Tall Paul ridicules Piggy's facing away from them and toward the toilet.

Zap has had enough. "Leave her be. She is showing some

compassion for a fallen fellow member and that's more than can be said for you."

In the background, the far away squeaking noise of Wee being crunched in the jaws of the hideous predator can be faintly heard. "Ohhh," moans 'C'.

Then, in unison, a crying human baby is also heard. "Bad dog!" is intoned by the father. "Give me that toy!" A long drawn out squeaking moan is then heard and footsteps come toward the bathroom. Wee is thrown into the center of the tub unceremoniously.

"Oh my!" says Zap.

"How ignoble," says 'C'.

"Are you alright?" yells Bluey.

"My head hurts a little. I'm all slimy. But I don't think I have any puncture wounds," says Wee with a small voice.

"Well thank goodness for that!" says Piggy.

"We were all extremely worried," lies Falls.

"Really, you guys were worried about me?" hopes Wee, gaining strength.

"What do you think?" Tall Paul says coldly.

"Oh, I guess you weren't all that scared after all," says Wee.

"That is not true, son. Many among us were deeply concerned. We are very happy to see you in one piece," Piggy comforts Wee.

"Did you give that beast a shot or two at least?" questions Zap.

Wee giggles. "Oh, I don't think so. He is pretty big after all. I don't think he was too scared of me."

"Your squeaking was very mature," says Bluey. "Very professional. That smelly hound may well think twice next time he tries to run off with one of us."

"Thanks, guys. Thanks for caring." Wee sounds tired. His arms are twisted oddly, with one wrenched behind his back. He tries to swing it around but cannot and is exhausted by the effort. He sleeps deeply, like a baby.

Tall Paul whispers to Falls, not wanting the others to hear. "That little squirt seems fine. Not even dented. I thought it was curtains for him. I saw the balance of power shift with us being the favorites as we rightfully should be."

Falls concurs. "Our time will come. You know how kids are. One day it's Superman, the next Spiderman. It's kind of funny to see his arms all messed up for a change, like he's about to fling something."

On the other side of the tub, Bluey and 'C' are speaking. "Unscathed. It's a miracle," says Bluey.

"I was scared to death. If that had been me—" 'C' shudders.

"The resilience of the young," continues Bluey.

'C' nods, still shaken as she watches Wee sleep peacefully.

Later that night, near the middle of it to be more precise, the nails of the dog's feet are heard clicking along the floors, roaming the house. And then once again, he is heard coming toward the bathroom. The dog stealthily prowls into the room, the sharp clatter of the nails on linoleum jarring the quiet night.

All the toys are awake, shivering at the thought of another among them being kidnapped and brutalized. The great sniffing nose pokes them and leaves wet spots on their sides from its prodding. All hold their breath, hoping the creature will lose interest.

Seemingly with malice of purpose, the great beast grabs Tall Paul with a mighty thrust as Tall Paul's loud protest SQUEAK echoes throughout the room. The dog carries Tall Paul from the room as the horrible high-pitched protest continues until it is in a far corner of the house, dim yet desperately sharp.

"Not again!" screams 'C'. "My heart can't take this abuse."

Falls is sobbing as she was right next to Tall Paul. She can't speak and is having a hard time catching her breath.

"Let's not panic, fellow toys," Piggy in her sage wisdom begins. "Wee was returned unhurt. Our experience shows us that this dog is a brute but not a killer."

Falls catches her breath. "Pipe down, you pacifist! We have to do something! Our leader is at this moment being tortured! Oh, the horror! What will we do?"

"You were certainly less concerned when it was Wee," says Bluey.

Wee looks up, shaking. "Really?"

"Look, Wee, wake up and smell the coffee. Those two other baby-shaped toys don't give a squeak about you. Your only friends among us are the oddities such as myself," notes Zap.

"They were hoping you were destroyed," cries 'C'.

Piggy tries to calm the rising hysteria. "They were scared like the rest of us. We are all helpless children, unable to properly defend ourselves. We have to believe that everything will turn out alright."

"Why, what good will that do?!" laments Falls.

"Let's try to get some sleep," says Zap. "Maybe the beast will tire of his cruel game and leave the bully alone."

"The Bully!?" cries Falls. "Where's your respect for authority? I can't sleep while he is out there somewhere, helpless in the jaws of that, that terrorist."

"I can sleep just fine if you'll just pipe down," says Bluey. "Goodnight all and hope for the best."

"Where's the humanity?!" cries Falls to deaf ears.

"Get your rest, Falls. You may need it," Piggy reminds her of the reality of an uncertain future.

Deep down, none among them is sorry that it was Tall Paul that was abducted. None among them would be missed less.

The morning bath did not bring Tall Paul back, as all had expected. In fact, neither the mother nor the child is aware that he is not among the toys. Wee is fondled and made over after his own ordeal, but it does not go unnoticed by the pack that Tall Paul is not once mentioned by the family.

The others manage to actually enjoy their bath experience, all except Falls who sulks and refuses to squirt the water from her airhole upon request. She is subsequently dropped in the water and allowed to fall to the bottom and left there, ignored, for the duration of the bath.

That evening, Tall Paul still has not been returned. All of them fear the worst: mutilation, mauling, disfigurement, large gaping holes in his limbs, the recycle bin. Little is said among them. Falls coughs to remove the water and sniffles.

Toward the morning Falls clears her throat to draw the attention of her fellow bath toys. Somberly she says, "Since it appears that Tall Paul has been dispatched to toy heaven, I feel that I am rightfully the new leader. I want you all to know that I have your best interests at heart—"

"Excuse me?" says Bluey.

"Who do you think you are?" joins 'C'.

"I don't believe we need a leader. A leader in this tribe in the past has meant only the loudest complainer and the most physically abusive bully," Piggy says sagely.

"Amen, sister," says Zap.

Falls continues. "I am the logical heir to Tall Paul. I will continue his reign as he would have wanted. Anyone who objects can deal with me."

"Well, you're going to have to deal with us. I nominate Piggy to be the new leader!" cries Bluey.

"Oh, I really don't see myself—" Piggy starts but she is interrupted.

"All for Piggy and Piggy for all!" cries Zap.

"Pig-gy, Pig-gy, Pig-gy, Pig-gy, Pig-gy, Pig-gy, Pig-gy, Pig-gy!" they all chant.

"Speech!" they yell in unison.

"Now all of you know we don't need a leader," Piggy begins. "We can all be here together without someone being stronger or more popular or another being the brunt of jokes. Why can't we come to each other for advice without fear that someone will criticize? Why set someone up among us as being better or more worthy? Why can't we all be directors on the Board of Bath Toys with equal voting power and equal say? Why can't we all be friends, or even a family?"

There is a loud uproar with whistling and squeaking and cheering for Piggy. Falls looks glum and sulky.

"Bad boy! Give that to me!" The mother's voice is heard from down the hall, rising above the tumult in the bathroom. "Oh, it's nearly ruined." She walks into the bathroom and unceremoniously throws a shapeless pink lump into the tub. It is a beaten up Tall Paul with a humbled and pained look on his face.

He is a broken toy. One foot is nearly severed. He has several deep punctures, one near his cheek. No one says anything. Falls breaks the silence.

"Are you alive?"

"Hello, everyone. Don't get up. I can't squeak any more, but yes, I am alive. How bad do I look?"

"Rather bad, I'm afraid," says Zap.

"You don't want to know," says 'C'.

"You look just fine," says Piggy.

They all turn to her, aware that this is extremely inaccurate. However, they realize that they must put their hearts where their mouths were just moments ago.

"Oh, really just a few scratches," starts Bluey.

"Surely, it's hardly noticeable," continues Zap.

"You just need a good bath," says 'C'.

"Good as new! New and improved! Keep out of reach of children!" pipes up 'Z'.

They all laugh, even Falls, at this outburst from 'Z'. Tall Paul has tears of joy and humility in his eyes. He lets the tears run down his face, one lodging in a puncture wound. "It's a cruel world out there, but not in here," he says. "In here it's kind and warm and a guy can feel special, even when he's not."

"No more talk like that," says Piggy. "We're all special. If we weren't, we wouldn't be here at all."

Everyone nods in agreement. "We're here because we're special and we're special because we're here," says Bluey.

In unison, making it clear to all that this new cheer will replace the old way of criticizing and emphasizing the differences between them, they begin to repeat Bluey's chant. "We're here because we're special and we're special because we're here," can be heard in the bathroom of the house in the suburb of a large metropolis if you listen very carefully.

Barbie Was Always Really Smart

Barbie was always really smart. Her mother, Esther, didn't figure she would be and named her after the doll. Esther loved Barbie dolls, even though she was a little old for them when they came out. Barbie was conceived in the euphoria following her mother buying a vacuum from a traveling salesman who kept right on traveling after their afternoon together. Her mother tried to track him down through the vacuum company, but they must have had inquiries of this nature before and said all that information was personal and confidential. So, neither Barbie nor her mother really knew Barbie's father.

Barbie and Esther had some hard times together after she was born. Before that, they got along fine. Esther never really had to develop any skills before Barbie came along, but becoming a mother has a way of accelerating one's development in general. She became a whiz at diaper changing and wiping spittle off a baby's face, and cleaning and washing and just about all of the essentials. However, she was unable to parlay these attributes into a paying job, so they were always broke. She worked for a few years watching the neighbor's kids while the neighbor went to work, but when that family moved away and Esther actually had some time to herself, she determined that gainful employment wasn't all it was cracked up to be.

They lived in an old house that Esther's father god-rest-his-soul had left her upon his demise. It was paid for by this time, mercifully, but the taxes and upkeep were a bitch. Consequently, it had an abandoned look with little curb appeal. The neighbors wondered why Esther didn't just sell the house to someone who would fix it up and turn around and sell it and make a killing so that the other property values on the street would go up, but Esther was born there and so was Barbie, and Esther wouldn't consider selling. As long as she could scrape up the money to keep them afloat month to month, which was never easy given Esther's lack of ambition, well, they were going to stay.

Also, the school system in which they lived was quite good. Esther didn't initially set too much store by this, since she figured Barbie's dad and mom weren't much in the brains department, but when Barbie started to show some promise in kindergarten, she had to change her mind. Not that Barbie would find a man through her brains, because no girl found a decent husband this way, not one Esther would find acceptable anyway. She would have to be cute to be noticed and then if she was smart, well, that would only make it all a little easier. Esther was all for anything that could make one's life easier. She expected that Barbie would find a rich husband so that Esther could move in with them but have her own wing or suite or whatever it was called, so that she could see them every day and visit the nursery, but then shut the door and have some peace and quiet once in a while. This was really all she lived for, and every day in her own quiet way, she was grooming Barbie for this happy inevitability.

From her first day in school, Barbie took a liking to it. She felt that that was where she belonged and for a while was angry with her mother for cheating her out of a real education in her early years at home. Rather than teaching her to read, Esther and Barbie watched late night reruns of old Doris Day and Annette Funicello movies. Rather than taking Barbie to something educational, they went to the track. Rather than buying her Lincoln Logs or letter blocks or anything with a hint of a learning-oriented bent, Esther bought her dolls and party dresses and ribbons. Barbie could have learned several foreign languages in all that time that was now lost, wasted, she thought. Well, she wasn't about to waste any more time. She always tried to do extra credit, stay after school and help the teacher, always asking questions as she helped restack the blocks. "I think there's more to it than you're telling me," she would implore. The teachers often didn't know quite what to do with Barbie. She was a special child. "Why can't we have more hours in school and less at home?" she wondered of her teachers. At first the school was fearful that she was having real trouble at home, but when it was apparent that Barbie was Barbie and Esther was Esther, and god knows exactly how that happened genetically, they just gave her extra work to do and tried to keep her busy. She skipped first grade, which Esther was initially against. She worried that it might cause emotional problems down the road, but somehow the principal convinced her that it would actually benefit Barbie to be on a higher intellectual and emotional plane than her current grade level classmates. Esther also worried that it might convince Barbie that school and good grades were rewarded more than a good marriage. But she thought that was too far away, and Barbie had plenty of time to realize all that for herself, as Esther knew she would as soon as she was exposed to it.

Esther tried to dress Barbie in clothes that were not age-appropriate for elementary school. She wanted her to wear midriffs and shorts to school when Barbie felt more comfortable in khakis and flannel shirts. Again, Esther felt the gnawing pang of fear, realizing that this would not do and did not fit in her plans. No worthwhile husband was interested in a woman in flannel shirts. They had quite a few arguments about this, but agreed to compromise after Esther saw how willful her daughter could be, figuring this was something she got from her father, and Barbie could have both of these types of clothes in her closet and would alternate styles. On the days of clothes of Esther's choosing, Barbie was not herself all day. She was always tugging at her shirt or skirt trying fruitlessly to lengthen it. She would not raise her hand in class, even if she knew the answer, for fear that too much skin would show on her side and stomach. She wouldn't draw any attention to herself in general, and even didn't speak to her friends unless spoken to. She felt that everyone was looking at her and, in reality, they were. She didn't look right. It was as if she was a doll, put on display by some larger hand, not a real human being with a personality and free movement and the choice not to be made to look ridiculous. But on the days when she could choose her own outfit, which she tried to slip in an extra one here and there, she showed the first signs of who she would ultimately become. She was competitive and willful and strong and funny and self-assured and somewhat selfish and the smartest kid in the class. She challenged the teachers and asked thoughtful questions that sometimes they had to get back to her on.

Barbie had lots of friends, especially girl friends, and was the class leader. She never invited anyone back to her house to play, always insisting that they went to the park or someone else's house. It wasn't the house in its decay that she was embarrassed about, but more and more as she grew up, her mother caused her soul wrenching humiliation. Now this is a fairly common complex of emotions among young people toward their parents, but in Barbie's case, she found her mother unacceptable. She did not want to put herself in a situation in which she would have to explain her mother to anyone. Most of her friends were not familiar with women like Esther, nor were many other people, for that matter.

As Barbie entered middle school, they grew further and further estranged. She never went to her mother with social or emotional issues, rarely showed her any of her schoolwork or things she worked on outside of school. Barbie joined the debate team and swim team so that she could spend less and less time with Esther. Barbie's grades were consistently excellent, so Esther didn't need to be checking on her, but Esther was realizing more and more that Barbie was not the girl she had expected when she was expecting.

One day at a parent-teacher conference with Barbie's seventh grade teacher—a woman of pretty good girth and androgynous features—Esther, who was wearing a non-age-appropriate outfit herself, a very scary, truly terrifying germ of a thought took purchase in Esther's brain. Naw, she dismissed it immediately, not her Barbie. Barbie was cute and adorable and teeny and feminine, she argued with herself. The teacher explained that Esther would have to give her permission for Barbie to take a sex education class, but that it was standard procedure and all of the other kids would be taking it.

"Will you be teaching the class?" Esther inquired.

"Yes, I will."

Barbie was the only kid in her seventh grade who had to go to the principal's office during the sex education classes. She was mortified by her mother's refusal, but in reality, all the kids knew about sex by now anyway. It was just the exclusion that she hated. Also, this was her favorite teacher and she would have liked to have heard it all it from her, instead of from clinical books and horny boys and Penthouse magazine, which is what happened.

Esther noticed Barbie's moping attitude after this episode and interpreting it incorrectly, decided to teach Barbie about sex herself. She drew some diagrams that made Barbie blush and explained where babies come from and how horrible childbirth is and how a penis can make a girl feel pretty good if the guy knows what he's doing and that her father got an A in that department, and how she missed it terribly, but that she didn't want to get a reputation in town so she was discreet, and how birth control was for career girls and she certainly didn't want to be one of those because they never have any boyfriends and that if you want to be popular you really should act like you know a lot about sex and she was definitely going to have to learn to flirt but Esther wasn't worried because she knew Barbie was a quick learner and at this point Barbie couldn't take it any longer and burst into tears, something she rarely did.

"Well, what is it my honey lamb?" Esther asked completely clueless.

"Mom, you're making me sick. This isn't sex education, it's child abuse. I'm going to my room to study. I have a test tomorrow."

That was the last time Esther felt that she connected with Barbie. In truth, she hadn't connected with Barbie since the umbilical cord was severed.

It all went more or less down hill after that. Barbie spent a lot of time at school, especially in the company of the teacher who eventually came out to the faculty as a lesbian and was, as was politically correct at the time, congratulated for her honesty and honored with a dinner for being the first at the school. Esther started hanging out in bars, and one day Barbie walked in on a strange man in the bathroom when she got up in the morning to get ready for school. The man smiled all wrong at Barbie and Barbie slammed the door and told him to knock once on the door when he was done. He did and when she opened the door again, he was still in there, smiling again. After that, Barbie held a mirror under the crack in the door to see if the coast was clear before she went into the bathroom.

College was always uncharted territory between Barbie and Esther. Esther felt that there was no need to discuss it since it didn't exist, and even though Barbie knew Esther felt this way, she also knew that she was going. She secretly researched colleges at the library and figured she could go pretty much anywhere she wanted. She knew she could get a grant since they were poor and she was smart and she could write damn good persuasive essays. So she started to do that, honing her essays to college X and Y long before she needed to submit any test scores or applications. She just didn't want to leave anything undone or done at the last minute, which would leave room for error. She had her essay complete and rewritten to the point of perfection by her sophomore year. All of her teachers encouraged her and knew she would have no trouble getting into college.

However, they did not understand, could not understand, the obstacle of Esther. It would be impossible to describe this impediment to almost anyone. And the reason she was such an impediment, because she wanted Barbie to marry a rich man so she, Esther, could live in a nice house and go shopping with someone else's money, well, that would have been tough to explain to one's average high school teacher who figures every parent wants her child to succeed on her own merit and terms. It was a given that the desire of every parent for her child was to see the child go out in the world prepared to meet any challenge, and that this would be immensely satisfying to that parent. Barbie tried to pretend in her own mind that Esther was her loony aunt, sadly afflicted with a rare dementia at a young age, who lived in the belfry with pet bats and that her father had been a gentle, noble non-celibate monk who had taken pity on her and tried to enlighten her, but failed and left, always hoping for the best.

The inevitable implosion came the summer between Barbie's junior and senior year of high school. At this point, Barbie, an intelligent, wise beyond her years, budding sexual woman had more than an inkling that she was gay and college bound. She felt that she could no longer keep this crucial information from her mother, who deserved a chance to go on with her life and try to find a rich man on her own. She needed to understand that Barbie would not be supplying the acceptable husband nor the 1.75 grandkids and the sooner it all came out in the open, well, the better for everyone. Barbie knew it would not be pleasant, and prepared for the day for months. She tried to apply intellect to the problem, looked at it as a mathematical equation that surely was solvable, maybe a logic problem and she studied Zen Buddhist riddles for weeks hoping to find an answer. In the end, she blurted it out over a dinner she had made of tofu and eggplant which already wasn't going over well.

It just came out during an argument over staying after school to take some college placement tests that Barbie had called IQ tests so as to not arouse any suspicion in Esther, but Esther wasn't born yesterday and was starting to put two and two together, even though she had already had several cocktails. It was a horrible row and in the end, everyone got hurt. Barbie ended up with a black eye, Esther with a broken heart and shattered dreams. Esther cried for weeks, the sorrow she felt for herself seemed bottomless. She visited a psychic who told her that her lifeline was awfully short and no need to panic, but there had been some kind of psychic break in her life and she needed to mend it. "How?" Esther wondered eagerly, but the psychic had no answer and charged her twenty-five dollars anyway. No one could comfort her and for the first time in her life, she turned to god for some sign. When no significant interpretable sign appeared to Esther on the next day, nor that second day she promised herself she would wait, sure that her patience would be rewarded, even looking for patterns in her coffee grounds and the mud she tracked in, she lost hope.

Being inconsolable, Esther went to the bar every night now, and became a raving, vengeful, bitter, nasty drunk. She had cheap sex in the alley behind the bar for drinks and change. Had Barbie known this, she may have pitied her mother, she may have tried to make her see that they could still have a life together, but that it would be more along the lines of what Barbie wanted, not Esther. Things had changed, and Barbie was willing to acknowledge her mother's part in her life and her sacrifices, and move forward from there. Had she noticed that her mother was a chronic alcoholic, she might have sought help for her, found a local AA chapter, even attended meetings with her. Had she had any sympathy for her mother's dead dreams, she may have stopped looking the other way and focused for a moment on the needs of this ailing, sad woman and opened her heart. She may have overcome her embarrassment and reached out, asking her mother's advice on housekeeping or colleges or even considered staying in the general area to be near her.

And had Esther shaken herself from her drunken self-pity she might have appreciated what a strong and charming and remarkable woman she had raised. She may have had a lasting sense of satisfaction in knowing that she was partly responsible for the genes and decisions that made her and that Barbie's existence justified her own. She might have chosen to live near Barbie and have a presence in her life, and perhaps share in her triumphs.

But none of this happened and Barbie went on to a successful career as a professor of applied mathematics at Bryn Mawr and had a series of meaningful monogamous relationships with wonderful women that were fulfilling for both of them and helped them to grow spiritually and move toward enlightenment to some degree and Esther died alone at home one night watching a Doris Day movie on TV.

Don't Make Me Hate You
(or, things that are said that just might)

We don't have to pretend anymore, we're married.

The concept of enlightenment just confuses me.

I wrote this hilarious standup routine about our relationship!

I like showing off my cleavage—if you've got it, flaunt it.

I love Jerry Springer!

So, how much weight *have* you gained?

I just don't think you're a size medium anymore.

This is the richest country on the planet. Why do we have to conserve anything?

Black and white photography is boring. It always seems like it needs some color.

I'm tired of trying to make my life better.

It's just simple economics. I'm paid more because I'm more valuable to society.

I'm going out to a strip club with the boys.

I guess I'm not a very good listener.

I'm not really that into keeping myself clean.

You're just like your father.

I never said you looked ugly exactly.

I wish it *was* a little bigger, now that you ask.

I'm on this new diet where I can't eat or drink anything until 8pm everyday.

If I could have dinner with anyone, it would be Demi Moore.

I guess I don't trust you to do it right.

I wish I had a fetish!

I guess I'm just a nobody.

I don't want to give you an ultimatum or anything, but when are we getting married?

You're starting to get a lot of wrinkles.

I thought I would part it low and brush it all over to one side to hide my male pattern baldness.

I don't need to learn how to use a computer. They're just a fad.

Can you get dinner? I left my wallet at home again.

Can you do some work on my car again this weekend?

I don't have any skills.

You're just going to have to accept me because I'm not changing.

I've given up trying to figure out what to do with my life.

I know I forgot your birthday, but you should have reminded me.

I was crazy about you from the moment our eyes met.

How many years have we been together again?

Let the maid do it.

I left your sunroof open during the storm last night.

Responsibilities just overwhelm me.

Marijuana leads to harder drugs, it's been proven somewhere.

How am I supposed to see someone else's side of the story?

Aren't you a little old for that hairdo?

Sometimes I just don't get you.

I was born to be on stage!

I don't believe in doing any recreational drugs and I don't need my mind expanded.

Don't be stupid.

Let's get rid of the cat.

They're just animals.

I was thinking about hiring a life coach to make me more 'hip'.

Legalize drugs, take the needle out of your arm!

My kids will always be the most important things in my life.

Work is always going to come first.

I'd rather watch sports all day.

I don't like to read.

My favorite color is flesh.

Well, how much can you loan me?

Are you kidding, it's great living at home—my mom takes care of everything.

I like to be babied when I'm sick.

My last girlfriend had huge tits.

Hey, sorry, when I told that joke I forgot your dad had been gored by a bull too.

I like to keep my toenails long.

I'm not asking, I'm telling you.

I asked you not to bug me when I'm watching TV!

To me, those people on 'Friends' are like my real friends.

What are you, chicken?

Well, she does have a nice butt!

I can't believe you're making such a big deal just because I dumped a beer over your head!

I told you I had a bad temper!

Well, success *is* a form of superiority.

You're just so naive.

You're crazy.

You're a nag.

You're a bitch.

I wish you were dead.

Fuck you.

Sometimes I can see why guys hit girls.

Maybe you need to double your dose cause it's not working.

No, I don't think I *have* had enough!

I don't want you to hang out with your friends anymore.

Come on, give me a smile.

Sometimes I really don't understand what you're talking about.

Where did you hear *that*?

You made me this way!

I think I might vote Republican this election.

Equal rights for women, what a joke!

Gay men kissing make me sick.

I can always join the army. I hear they're looking for people.

I only need five hours of sleep a night.

Get a life!

I could always sell drugs again.

I did the dishes last week.

I don't like to be touched during the night.

You're the fucked up one!

I don't know how to fix anything around the house.

I can only have sex with the lights out and most of my clothes on.

Are you on the rag?

I have enough friends so, if this doesn't work out, you can just lose my number.

Could you get up and get me another beer?

Let's watch some porno on the internet.

For me, this *is* being romantic.

I love stories about princes and princesses with happily-ever-after endings.

I think those fake ATM receipts that make it look like you have a lot of money in your bank account are excellent.

I was thinking of getting vaginal plastic surgery.

Are you kidding me—telemarketing is a great gig!

If I were you, I wouldn't be showing my legs.

I don't want to get my hair wet.

I could see getting those pectoral implants when I get older.

I'd rather be hunting.

It takes hours of work to get this natural look.

I'm just always really busy, that's all.

The rawer and bloodier my meat, the better.

I just don't understand what vegetarians eat.

Read my lips.

I'm a witch.

I just can't work with people.

I went over there a few times and looked in the window and did follow him once, but I wouldn't call it stalking.

I know I told you I was over it, but I think I might be gay again.

You are what you eat is just plain not true.

I was thinking of tattooing around my eyes so I won't have to use eyeliner anymore.

Are you kidding, mustaches look great on me.

Let's PARTY!

I'd rather fix you than work on myself.

I just don't want to be part of your struggle.

What's wrong with being judgmental? People are fucked up!

You don't make enough money for me.

I need a professional man.

Could you wear something sexy to impress my boss?

What about a threesome?

I hate your dog.

My dog hates you.

It's me or the dog.

Let's just be honest and say everything we don't like about each other.

You used to be hotter.

I used to care about your problems at work.

How can you be lonely, we're married?

I can't tell you what I really think, it would hurt your feelings.

Well, your feelings are stupid then.

I was thinking about starting a band in the basement.

I told you so.

Liposuction seems a hell of a lot easier than dieting.

What's ethics again?

I just like to watch movies that are entertaining. My own life is depressing enough.

Spicy food is too ethnic for me.

I'd like to go out in a blaze of glory.

It's always been this way and it's fine the way it is.

If it's not in the 'Rules' book, I don't do it.

Your voice annoys me sometimes.

I don't see the connection between the gas mileage of my Expedition and the war in Iraq.

I'm not buying a hearing aid! Just turn up the damn TV.

Could we please just not experiment with my dinner?

I painted it in kindergarten. I thought we could hang it in the bedroom.

I just wish we were invited to more Hollywood parties.

You kiss weird.

It's too confusing, keeping up with all the exploitation in the world.

Ignorance is bliss, believe me.

I never really got into oral sex.

I think it's time I settled down, bought a house, got married and had a few kids.

I love those planned, gated developments.

If we had to we could move in with my mom for a while.

I like to have the TV on all day as background noise.

Let's just forget about the date and go back to my house and screw.

I think guys that drive Humvees are cool.

Recycled paper isn't worth the extra quarter a ream to me.

What do *you* know? Maybe there's some global strategy behind the president of the US looking stupid.

You would have a great body with breast implants.

You look really good for your age. How old are you again?

I guess I'm just a meat and potatoes kind of guy.

America. Love it or leave it.

After all, it's not God Bless France!

I don't vote since they're all the same anyway.

It's Ralph Nader's fault Gore lost.

I can't believe you've never read any Socrates.

I don't see anything wrong with men making decisions about women's reproductive rights.

Don't you have any *cool* friends?

For a while I was into dating black chicks. Then it was Orientals.

You gotta strike back hard and fast or they'll think you're weak.

My Mom's a big fat miserable human being.

Your French accent is really northeast Montreal.

Dick Cheney is hot.

Henry Kissinger said 'Power is the ultimate aphrodisiac' and I tend to agree.

Food made from hemp? That's way too out there for me.

I don't believe in spirituality.

If you would just accept Jesus Christ as your personal savior everything would change in your life.

I don't do anything until I check my horoscope.

Bird watching is for doofesses.

Who'd want to ruin a good vacation doing something educational?

I can drive drunk.

I'm going to get a tattoo of CARPE DIEM across my back to remind myself of the shortness of our lives.

Earthquakes don't scare me.

Don't you ever just feel like driving off a cliff?

My last girlfriend said I gave her the creeps.

I started saving for my retirement in high school.

I don't want to go anywhere new.

George Bush is such a sincere speaker.

Let's go to EuroDisney when we're in Paris!

Don't use those big words on me!

Delayed gratification seems stupid, I mean, there's no guarantee I'll even be alive tomorrow.

I don't think there's anything wrong with being a perfectionist.

I hate asking for directions. Let's just try to figure it out.

Most people are just lying assholes.

Maybe this is below the belt, but I'm going to say it anyway.

You call it cruel, I call it honest.

Anything to save money!

Ever since I was a little kid I've wanted to work at Disneyland.

Yeah, I have a kid. Didn't I tell you?

I hate speaking during sex, and definitely no laughing.

I'll just declare bankruptcy again.

If you really loved me, you'd love my faults.

I don't think you can be too politically correct.

The last book I read was Bob Dole's autobiography.

Monica Lewinsky is hot!

Therapy is for losers who can't figure out their own problems.

I never run out of things to talk about.

Well, having a job in a sweatshop is better than no job at all!

Why would you want to be with me?

I'm just jealous because I care so much about you.

I can't think of anything you could tell me that would be a turn off.

I've never been to the dentist.

If you got cancer I'd probably bail.

I wanted to tell you I was married, but it just never came up.

Let's watch this great videotape I just bought of TV commercials!

If there's no parking, I just park in the handicapped space.

I just got us tickets to KC and the Sunshine Band!

If I don't have sex at least every other day I start looking around at other women.

I'm willing to lose a few civil liberties to keep this country safe from terrorism.

I don't need too many female friends since I consider myself a man's woman.

Just so you know, I've never had a monogamous relationship.

If I don't get flowers and candy on the first date, I won't see the guy again.

I'm just bummed that they won't be cloning people for spare body parts in my lifetime.

I never get tired of talking on the phone.

Do you think I'd look good with a pierced cheek?

I really don't want your opinion.

I love having a ton of gay friends.

I just wish you were smarter, that's all.

I knew you'd try to make me get a job.

Those high school days were the happiest of my life.

If I can pay for it, I should be able to have it.

Don't waste your time with that charity job since you'll never make a dent in the homeless population.

My one man show is about the how fucked up it is to pay money to watch someone perform live like a trained monkey.

I'm not really worried about the long-term survival of the human species. We've done all right so far.

Maybe it isn't fair, but when you say something, often I check your facts on the internet.

I really didn't believe Anita Hill.

Maybe I am cheap, but at least I'll have something when I retire.

My friends make fun of me, but I got license plates that reflect how I feel about myself: 'SUCSSFL.'

Only people who have something to hide care about being drug tested at work.

Peace and quiet is boring.

Maybe we should take separate vacations.

I think cliché means truth in French.

Why do you always want to change things? Let's just paint the walls the same white they were before.

You'll never get me on a plane again! If I can't drive there, I'm not going.

It's crazy to talk about quitting a job with those benefits!

I'd love a fur coat—the more exotic the better.

I think that a long pinkie fingernail looks cool on guys.

A board game party? That sounds stupid.

I think if you had understood it you would have liked it better.

Sometimes the word cunt just fits.

Do you *have* a good side?

You'd make a terrible mother.

I just can't relate to feminism anymore.

Oh yeah, make me!

Don't you ever just want to buy a gun and shoot something?

There is zero percent chance that there is life outside of our solar system.

I'm looking out for number one.

My psychic friend warned me about you.

I think we spend more than enough time together.

My guilty pleasure is Harlequin Romances.

I thought we could join a local 'Chicken Soup for the Soul' club.

I wish you weren't so friendly.

I don't need to know him since he doesn't make the big decisions.

Let's buy plastic plants. The real ones are just going to die.

I don't get what all the fuss is about. Trees are renewable, right?

You're so negative! It's not too late for me to become an astronaut.

We might as well just accept genetically altered foods as inevitable.

Who'd want to steal *my* identity?

What's Your Problem?

LOUD APPLAUSE

"Thank you very much ladies and gentlemen in our studio audience. And welcome viewers at home to *What's Your Problem?* the game show that attempts to do what it takes therapists years to do: figure out what's wrong with our contestants in twenty questions. Okay, let's meet our Celebrity Panelists. On my left is the newest hip-hop phenom singerslashactress, A-Ho."

The audience applauds wildly. A-Ho nods appreciatively. She is twentysomething, has great skin and wears a ton of makeup.

"And in the center, for experiential contrast, the bawdy old-time comic, Blue Buttons."

Less enthusiastic clapping, but there are some fans out there who still remember his day or else are regular show watchers.

"And since women are just plain better at asking the probing questions, our last panelist is also a woman. The renowned Psychic Friend, Evermora."

The audience seems to appreciate Evermora's additions to the show, if the applause is any indication.

"And I'm John Smith, the host of our show. Well, let's meet our contestant for today's show. We can't divulge too much about her, since that is part of the panelists' task, but according to the rules, I can tell you this much about 'Marjorie,' which is not her real name. She is a single 37 year-old middle-manager in Los Angeles. She has no children and has one sister and one brother. Her father is living, but her mother passed away two years ago. She owns her own home. She lives alone. Okay, then, let's meet 'Marjorie.'"

Lots of clapping for 'Marjorie' as she enters from off-stage. She is fairly tall and thin, medium blonde hair, dressed in a dark pants suit. She smiles, somewhat timidly at John Smith and then the panelists, imploring them with her eyes to go easy on her. She takes her seat off to the other side of the Celebrities. They can all see each other. The clapping subsides.

"Okay, according to our rules, we will start with the panelist on the right, A-Ho. Question number One."

"All right, Marjorie, do you like, have a boyfriend?"

Blue Buttons erupts. "You can't ask yes or no questions! All you're going to get is a 'yes' or a 'no' and how does that help us? We only have twenty questions, A-Ho!"

Marjorie says "Yes."

"See!" yelps Blue Buttons. A-Ho applies more lipstick.

"Blue Buttons, question number Two."

"Okay, to expand on the previous question, can you describe your relationship with your boyfriend? Go ahead, include any juicy details so I can live vicariously."

The audience laughs obligatorily to the flashing LAUGH sign.

Marjorie swallows hard, her Adams apple bobbing. Did someone not describe the show to her?

"Well, we've been together for about six months, and he's a really nice man, he's a few years older than me. He works in the building next door and we met eating lunch in the industrial park between the two buildings. He has two grown children who are in college." She looks to John Smith who motions to expand and raises his eyebrows encouraging her to juice it up. "Well, he stays at my house sometimes and I've stayed at his. It's very comfortable and we have common interests and he's actually a lot of fun. He likes to go to outdoor concerts—"

Evermora interrupts, hurrying her turn out of impatience. "How's the intimacy, my dear?" The audience claps without the sign.

Marjorie reddens slightly, but squares her shoulders. Apparently, she actually wants to find out what's wrong with her. "I enjoy his body. I hadn't had a ... sexual relationship for nearly a year before I met him, so I was ready."

The audience laughs and A-Ho spits up the soda she was drinking. "Anyway, he's very gentle and cares how I feel and well, it's very satisfying."

John Smith waits to see if she will continue, but she doesn't and he calls on A-Ho to ask question number Four.

"I can't believe you're only thirty-seven, girlfriend. Anyway, tell me about your first sexual experience."

Marjorie reddens further. "I'm not sure I know what you mean."

The camera pans to a woman seated in a glass booth wearing large earphones. John Smith consults this judge with his microphone turned off. The judge makes a verdict. "A-Ho, please expand upon the question so that your entire meaning is clear to the contestant."

"Okay, okay, what's the first sexual thing you remember about yoself?"

Marjorie squirms visibly.

"Well, this is a little embarrassing, but when I was a girl, and this is the first thing I can remember so there may have been something else, but anyway, the girl next door, who was a year older than me, well, we used to pull down our pants and look at each other's privates."

The audience is silent, thinking about what they would have to reveal about themselves if asked the same question. Someone in the audience holds up a sign that says, 'BORING'.

John Smith gives everyone a moment and then, "Blue Buttons, question number Five.

"Okay, well, that seems pretty normal, most of us did stuff like that when we were kids. Is there anything, unnatural, deviant, well, something that you fantasize about sexually?"

Marjorie ponders. "No," she finally says.

A-Ho jumps on this. "That was a yes or no question, Jack!"

"Okay, panelists, let's respect each other. Every question is a good one."

"Why didn't you say something when he dissed me?"

Blue Button waves to someone in the audience.

Ignoring A-Ho, John Smith turns to Marjorie and says, "Marjorie, remember what we discussed about revealing something traumatic and painful." He raises his eyebrows and nods his head in a paternalistic nudge.

"We'll be right back after this commercial message. Don't go away, folks."

The cameramen take drinks of water and coffee. A-Ho stands up and stretches and looks pouty as John Smith goes over to talk to her and Blue Buttons. Evermora adjusts her chair so that she is sitting up even straighter and does some deep breathing. Marjorie applies powder as if seeking general facial camouflage. John Smith signals that he is ready and things are smoothed over and he heads back in front of the cameras.

"We are back, folks, with more of *What's Your Problem?* Okay, Evermora, question number Six."

"Marjorie, please describe your childhood."

Marjorie looks more comfortable and spends a few minutes detailing her early years growing up in a Chicago suburb, being close with her Dad, but not her mother, since Marjorie felt her mother really didn't care for being a mother, playing with her brother and sister in the wading pool, enjoying reading at a young age, having her first boyfriend in second grade and him walking her home after school, her parents' occasional arguments over money and housecleaning.

A-Ho jumps in: "Yeah, but didn't you never have no fun?"

Marjorie looks hurt. "Well, sure, we were a pretty close family and we laughed a lot. I feel like I had a better childhood than most of my friends. Really, there were a lot of good times that I recall vividly."

Now Blue Buttons speaks up. "I think what A-Ho is getting at is, do you have any of the child from then still in you now?"

A-Ho retorts, "That really isn't what—" but she stops herself on a look from John Smith.

"I have lost a lot of that fun, I have to admit. I really loved being a child most of the time, and as an adult, well, a lot of that is gone. That passion and excitement for each new day, you know, that expectation that you have about your life when you're a kid, how great everything will be, well, I guess that's just part of growing up and maturing and taking responsibility for your life."

Another sign appears from an audience member: 'SEX IT UP'.

"Okay, Evermora, question number Nine."

"Marjorie, why are you here today?"

"That's a really good question. My friends sort of talked me into it because they said I would be the perfect candidate since I was so hard to figure out. They said that I had a pretty happy childhood and a good job and a good guy and I should be happier. Plus, I wanted to do some remodeling on my house and could use the money."

"A-Ho, number Ten, please."

"You can tell a lot about a girl by her choice of scent. What perfume do you wear, Marjorie?"

Blue Buttons rolls his eyes, but refrains from speaking, since he doesn't want the reciprocal criticism.

"Mostly I only wear perfume when I get dressed up, go out for the evening, but then I either wear White Diamonds or Chloe."

"Mmmmmmm," says A-Ho, writing something down.

"Very insightful," says Blue Buttons.

"Number Eleven," says John Smith.

"Well, it sounds like you have some problems with your Mom," starts Blue Buttons. "Can you describe your relationship with her a little further?"

"I loved my mom and all that, but when she died, I just didn't feel that much and wondered about that. We were so different. She didn't really care about my education; it was more about my brother all the time. He was more important. And she just always seemed like she would have enjoyed a different life. She wanted to go out and have fun and my dad wanted to stay home and barbeque. I think she just felt put upon by having these three kids and being stuck in the house. And spending your whole life doing something you don't want to be doing, well, I look at that as a waste of a life. You only get one chance, and I think she just, well, made a mess of it and that affected all of us. I think that's part of the reason I wasn't so keen on having kids myself and wanted a good job and to be independent. I saw her life and tried to do the opposite."

"Where is your spirituality, my dear?" intones Evermora.

"Well, I'm Episcopalian, go to church every few weeks. Is that what you mean?"

The Judge is consulted again and it is agreed that Evermora can expand her question.

"Tell us about how you view god."

Another sign comes up from the audience: 'SHOW US YOUR TITS!' Someone in the audience whistles at the sign. Marjorie doesn't look up and continues.

"I see God as a loving, kind being that sees all of us and wants the best for us and shows us the way through the bible and other teachings, but that we have to make our own decisions and our own mistakes and we will be judged one day for them. I feel that, in general, we will be forgiven our sins and mistakes if we try to do the right things."

That doesn't seem to fully satisfy Evermora, based on the frown on her face, but John Smith wants to move on. "Number Thirteen."

"Aren't you, like, creative, in any way?" A-Ho asks.

"I used to like to draw when I was a kid, but now, I'm too busy for lessons or anything like that. I enjoy decorating my house and I'm trying to be creative with that. I decided against all white walls when I recently repainted, for example. I thought that was sort of bold and creative."

The audience is getting restless. Signs are popping up saying: 'CAN HER' and 'HO HUM' and 'GIVE HER THE BOOT!' And a low grumbling has started.

"Fourteen."

Blue Buttons seems to be pondering something. "Did you ever have any kind of sense that your own life had no meaning?"

"Sure, I do. I wonder about that at times, doesn't everyone? I mean, going to college, getting a good job, finding a good husband, we grew up with all that like it would give us meaning. Mostly it does, but there are times that I wonder about it, I guess, you know, is this all there is?"

Blue Buttons nods, as if he has it figured it out. He writes for quite a while in his notepad.

John Smith looks out to the audience and hears the grumbling and sees the various signs. He turns to the THERMO-METER on the wall and points to it. It is in the 'Cold' section.

"Marjorie, if you notice, you are out in the 'Cold' still. If you don't make the audience warm up to you at least fifteen degrees by the end of the show, you will lose half of your winnings."

Marjorie shields her eyes from the glaring lights and squints in order to get a look at the THERMO-METER. It has only moved up ten degrees throughout the show. She nods her head, as if vowing to herself to do better.

"Have you ever felt any communication with your mother from beyond the grave?" Evermora wonders.

"Um, well, I would have to say no to that. I have occasionally had dreams about her, but nothing that has stuck with me." Marjorie looks disappointed and fearful for her money since she can't say that she has in order to suck the audience in.

"We're down to the final few questions, panelists, so think

carefully. Start honing your premise so that you can arrive at a conclusion when we take our next break."

"Did you ever want to have sex with a woman after having that hanky panky when you were a kid?" A-Ho asks.

"Oh no. I was really ashamed of it and I can't really believe I talked about it today. I have never told anyone, really. I am not interested in women that way, although I have a couple of great female friends and we're very close, and I have no problem whatsoever with lesbians or gays."

A-Ho writes furiously.

The THERMO-METER moves up five degrees with the acceptance of gays remark.

"Seventeen."

Blue Buttons is on to something. He looks intently at Marjorie. "When was the last time you felt really alive?"

Marjorie blushes. "Right now, I guess, under all this pressure. But before this, well, um, about a month ago I was thinking of taking a skydiving lesson and I researched it on the internet, and I came really close to doing it, so, that made me feel alive. But I got too scared at the last minute."

Evermora is also on to something. "Do you believe in Heaven and Hell?"

"I think I do. Especially Heaven, although I don't know about the clouds and white robes and all that. I think it is more a place the soul goes, to meet with god, after death, not a physical place." Marjorie nods, content with that answer.

"Number Nineteen, ladies and gentlemen, start formulating your answers."

A-Ho's final question. She squints at Marjorie. "Did your Dad ever touch you funny, that you can remember anyway?"

Blue Buttons groans. Marjorie winces. The audience perks up.

"No, absolutely not. I would have remembered that."

A-Ho interjects. "Sometimes you don't, honey, believe me."

"Okay, but I don't think it happened. Definitely not." Marjorie is done with that question.

The final question comes down to Blue Buttons. The tension is thick in the room. Marjorie is fearful and bites her nails.

Blue Buttons lifts his eyes from his notes. "Do you think of yourself as a good girl?"

Marjorie is taken aback by this. She stutters for a moment, then closes her mouth. Finally, she utters only the word "Yes" in a near whisper.

A-Ho glares at Blue Buttons.

Marjorie's 'temperature' on the THERMO-METER goes up ten degrees for the sympathy that one softly uttered word engendered in the audience.

"Okay panelists, that is all the information you will be given to determine what is Marjorie's lifelong problem, her Achilles heel, her fatal flaw if you will. Now in addition, you are asked to help her to solve this problem. Each one of you will analyze her problem, then give her the solution to change her life. After that, the audience votes on which one they most agree with. And finally, our expert psychoanalyst, who has been listening offstage, will offer the actual analysis, and Marjorie will hopefully go on to use all of this information to improve herself. So, don't change that dial, we'll be right back!" John Smith reads all of this from a cue card. His smile fades as the cameraman lets him know he has stopped filming.

A-Ho shields her notes from Blue Buttons, who moves his chair further from hers. Evermora closes her eyes and breathes rhythmically, her eyes moving back and forth beneath their lids.

LOUD APPLAUSE

"Okay, then, we are back with the results from our panelists. This is the most exciting part. All right, let's start with Evermora. Your analysis of Marjorie please."

Evermora opens her eyes and speaks slowly, authoritatively. "I believe that Marjorie has no real sense of her own power, her own higher power, and places all of the strength in her life in a male-centered god that is benevolent when one is good and punishing when one is bad. She says that she sees herself as good, but she seems to resent that she has not been 'rewarded' for that good behavior. She has not embraced her own power within and therefore, she sees herself as powerless to seek change and find true meaning. The solution lies in expanding her own spiritual plane through meditation, retreats, yoga, learning about other religious beliefs and basically expanding her own heart and mind through the knowledge that she is beautiful and unique and limitless."

The audience claps warmly.

John Smith smiles. "Didn't the woman three days ago have that same problem, Evermora?"

"Nearly everyone has this problem, I'm afraid," Evermora sighs deeply.

"All right then, Blue Buttons, your opinion of Marjorie's problem."

"It's very clear to me that Marjorie has thought all her life that if she is a good girl and does the right thing and is useful and all that jazz, that she will be happy and fulfilled and have a meaningful life. But we all know that's crap. You are not rewarded by society for these things, for being 'good'. You are rewarded and achieve greatness by risk-taking and aggressiveness and taking the road less traveled and feeding the old ego. So, basically, I think she needs to take that skydiving lesson and take painting classes and have a lot of sex and just do it! Just get out there and seize life by the balls. You only regret those things you don't do, believe me." He winks at the audience knowingly.

The audience claps warmly for this too. Blue Buttons looks pretty sure of himself, the epitome of a man who has done it all and not regretted it, although he *is* a Celebrity Panelist on a game show, after all.

"Okay, lastly, Miss A-Ho. Your opinion of Marjorie's problem."

"Miss Marjorie has some big problems if you ask me. She is repressed, girl. I see that she was repeatedly molested by her father when she was a little girl and it is now a repressed memory that she is repressing. I think because of this, she turned gay and now is wanting to be with other girls and can't admit it. The solution is to come out, start dating girls, get hypnotized to really go deep in there and write a tell all book about her Dad and all that and *cleanse*. She'll have money to quit her depressing job and she can come clean with herself and start to have some fun, girlfriend."

The audience claps wildly. The CLAP-O-METER arm points to A-Ho's analysis.

"Well, there you have it, the audience thinks A-Ho's analysis is the correct one. Well, let's bring out our expert, Psychoanalyst Doctor Alfred."

The audience clapping continues and accompanies Doctor Alfred's entrance. He nods. He is old and wizened and seems to exude lots of books he must have read about psychology.

"Welcome, Doctor Alfred. So, you've been listening backstage, tell us if any of the panelists are right."

"I have to say, there is a bit of truth in what the panelists say, but basically, they are all incorrect in their analysis of Marjorie."

Marjorie jumps up, elated. A neon dollar sign flashes above her.

"Well, that's good news for Marjorie since if no one is correct, if she stumps them so to speak, she makes an extra ten thousand dollars. And since she managed to rustle up the needed fifteen degrees on the THERMO-METER, she gets to keep it all, well, except for the hefty taxes. All right then, Doctor Alfred, what is your expert opinion of Marjorie's problem?"

"John, I believe that Marjorie is deeply afraid of failure because of how she views her mother. To Marjorie, in her own words, her mother's life was 'wasted'. But by judging others to be less than ourselves we makes ourselves feel better. Marjorie used her mother's 'failures' to showcase her own 'successes'. So therefore, due to the nature of a psychological complex, Marjorie is deeply connected to her mother's failure and by her own fear of it, she is actually fueling failure within herself. She is keeping her mother's failure alive by desperately trying not to be one herself so consequently, she has become one. That is what the complex does, it draws you inexplicably toward that which you fear the most. She has kept her emotional dependency upon her mother's failure harbored within her so that she would not be totally ostracized from her own family and from the child within herself that sought their approval. The solution is to fully understand how this has happened within her over the years and to break the cycle. This may require years of therapy, perhaps through www.doctoralfred.com, but it is necessary to become a fully-developed personality."

The audience claps loudly, but not as loudly as it did for A-Ho. Marjorie looks perplexed, but happy, as she watches the dollar sign above her head add up her winnings. A-Ho shakes her head, not knowing what Doctor Alfred was talking about. Blue Buttons claps for Doctor Alfred, who is also his own therapist, and Evermora looks at her watch.

"Well, that's it, folks, another life saved thanks to *What's Your Problem?* I'd like to thank A-Ho, look for her next blockbuster, the remake of *Gone With the Wind*, coming this summer; Blue Buttons can be seen most weekends at the Sands in Vegas; and Evermora can be found by dialing 1-800-PSYCHIC. I'm John Smith. Tune in tomorrow for 'Pete,' not his real name, who comes to us from rural Tennessee and just isn't having much luck with girls. Until then, keep looking at yourself in the mirror and asking '*Why?*'"

LOUD APPLAUSE

Pitch Man

My husband and I were having problems in our marriage of the delicate nature. It took months of gentle discussions and cajoling to get him to consider the possibility of making an appointment with a therapist. He wanted recommendations from several unaffiliated sources and a bio and resume and testimonials. He relented after a hissy fit from me and a discreet recommendation from our family physician.

Dr. Hilton was the name of the man we settled on. We didn't know at the time that our longtime family physician and Dr. Hilton went to college together and had several joint business ventures. I guess we would have gone anyway, had we known. Their business was really none of our business.

My husband is what is now known as old school. That's what comes from mixing no school and old age. Not that we're that old, but age is in the mind too. And our minds were brittle. They were encrusted. The only hair-like growth on their pates was mold. And I was not about to spend our remaining years on earth avoiding vitality. My husband eventually came around to see this also. But by the time we went to see Dr. Hilton, most of my energy for the process had been used up in trying to convince my husband to go at all. I was already worn down and vulnerable. Perhaps that lack of a guard dog was perceived by the slick Dr. Hilton.

I should have known by the office décor that this was not the man for us. I can only describe it as professionally decorated. It was not homey. It was not inviting. Our friends did not have professionally decorated houses and we wouldn't feel comfortable in them if they suddenly came into money and could actually hire a professional decorator. I sat on the edge of my chair, waiting to be called into the office by the secretary that evidently used Pert Plus. A man opened the door from the doctor's office and immediately shut it behind him as he entered the waiting area. He spoke to the secretary in very hushed tones, looking pretty dejected I thought, and left without looking at us. I swallowed. My husband looked straight ahead. I swallowed again.

Dr. Hilton was sitting at his desk when we entered, but stood to shake our hands—my husband's first in deference. A television was on directly behind his head, so you couldn't help but see it, even though the volume was down low. 'So clients feel at home' was what Dr. Hilton said in explanation.

After general pleasantries, we got down to business. How much was this going to cost, my husband wanted to know. That took a bit of time in determining how much insurance would cover and for how long. When it was determined that we could have twenty free visits, my husband relaxed and I knew it was because he figured we wouldn't need nearly that many.

'Mrs. ——, Dr. Hilton started smoothly, 'Please explain to me what you are hoping to achieve through the therapy process.'

They always go for the woman first, I thought. He could see that my husband was stiff and sweating and his only hope lay in getting me to break the ice for him.

'I can only say that I want our lives to be better,' I stammered. 'I want things to improve. I want to be happier. I want my husband to talk to me.'

While I was talking, I noticed that Dr. Hilton was fiddling with the various things on his desk, arranging them so that all of the brand names faced out toward us. The logos on his Coke can, his stapler, his pen, his cell phone, his mouse pad that advertised the brand of his computer were all now legible to us. I only noticed because I wanted to focus on something. It just seemed like a nervous habit of his at the time.

'Mr. ——, do you want these same things?'

My husband stared at me blankly. 'I guess.'

'Well, good, that's excellent. We have a place to start. You both want to talk about bettering your life. That sounds like a good place to end it for the day, since the fifty minutes are nearly up. Why don't we say same time next week, and during the upcoming week, why don't you both discuss the progress we made today? I'm just very pleased that we are all on the same page.'

As he led us out the door and into the hallway, he whistled. It sounded like several repetitions of 'Have you driven a Ford, lately?', the jingle from a television commercial.

My husband expected to be lauded simply for showing up to the appointment for the entirety of the next week. He was demanding and disagreeable and stubborn and refused to speak about our 'progress' as we had been instructed. I became sulky and depressed.

'How are we today?'

Dr. Hilton looked at me, of course. I shook my head without saying anything. My husband said, 'She's been crabby. Worse than usual.'

'Mrs. ——, are you feeling depressed?'

'Maybe a little,' I managed.

'Aren't you happy that you are here?'

'I guess.'

'Have you ever taken anti-depressants?'

'No.'

'Do you want to?'

'I'm not a drug person.'

'No one is a drug person until they actually take drugs, Mrs. ——.'

'I never thought of it that way.'

'I'll give you a prescription for Prozac, since that seems to be very popular. Then we'll see if you snap out of it. And maybe this will help.'

He reached into his drawer and pulled out several brochures with beautiful glossy pictures of white beaches and palm trees and tall glass-and-stucco pastel-colored condominiums.

'Do you know anything about time-shares? Maybe a good regular vacation spot where the staff knows your name and the breeze whispers softly while you enjoy a tall cool drink while watching the palms sway would do you two a world of good.'

My husband didn't speak again the entire session. I got a prescription for happy pills and brochures for a time-share in Mexico.

'Do you think it's working?' my husband asked.

'What?'

'The pills and the therapy.'

'Too soon to tell,' I said. I wanted to be patient. It had only been a couple of weeks. But the time-share seemed like a better and better idea every day.

After we signed up for the time-share for one week a year, Dr. Hilton seemed to take more interest in our case. One day, we even talked about something important.

'We don't have much intimacy any more. We're kind of like roommates,' I blurted out one day when I was feeling bold and entitled to be disgruntled.

'We had our day,' my husband said.

'That was yesterday, another era. What about today?'

'You expect too much.'

'You expect too little.'

'Well, I'm not going to be running after you no more. Those

days are done.'

Dr. Hilton reached into his drawer and pulled out a small bottle of blue pills. 'Not so fast, Mr. ——, happy days are here again.'

It took a few more weeks of proving to my husband that drugs work before he would take the blue pill. And then, afterward, there was the shame and embarrassment of shared intimacy after so long. I felt like I had slept with another man. We couldn't look at each other for the two days before our next appointment.

'It's okay to feel.' Dr. Hilton saw right away that we had a case of the heebie-jeebies of each other. A reaction to the blue pill.

'It feels weird,' I said.

'Be careful what you wish for,' my husband piped in.

While my husband talked about his job for the rest of the session—we didn't get any further with the intimacy discussion—I watched part of an infomercial on a Bellybuster on the TV behind Dr. Hilton's head. When he noticed I was watching, he turned up the volume.

After about twelve sessions, I had a Bellybuster and my husband wore a wrist band for his carpal tunnel syndrome (diagnosed by Dr. Hilton) and we had been to the time-share and Dr. Hilton's wife's Tupperware parties and we had bought a new Ford and both of us were taking drugs regularly and we were getting used to the awkward couple of days after we had sex with the blue pill and we had some hot stock tips we needed to talk to our broker about and we got a few extra free sessions for referring some friends and we refinanced our house through Dr. Hilton's mortgage broker to pay for all the new goodies while we waited for the settlement that was sure to come for the carpal tunnel syndrome.

My husband thinks our life is better now. I guess I don't feel quite as hopeless as I used to. He thinks when our 20th session is over we might even pay for a few more ourselves. He says the new car makes him feel snazzy. He even makes sexual jokes once in a while, which embarrasses more than excites me. I don't think we really talk any more than we used to, but we don't seem to get on each other's nerves quite so much. I feel a little taken sometimes when I think how much longer I will have to remain working to pay for this better life, especially with my husband on disability, and I wonder where Dr. Hilton's loyalty lies. When our family physician who recommended Dr. Hilton sent us a Christmas card for the first time this year it made me even more suspicious.

The warning signs were all there. We made a choice to not see. Now, when we enjoy life and eat out more often, we know we're being manipulated, but we go anyway. My husband says we have a better life now through advertising and products. I guess as long as it's better I should just be quiet and keep taking my pills.

Clean For a Day

Helen was not a clean freak. She was a normal, healthy, dirt-disliking person. What happened to her you wouldn't wish on the worst person you know.

It all started when Helen finally had enough money to get her own place with Sparky, her large, hairy dog. She needed a house with a yard because of Sparky, so she had lived with her neat freak, forever-scrubbing-something mother in the suburbs since she graduated from college to save up the money to move to something acceptable. She had tolerated her mother's fanaticism, but as was stated earlier, she herself was a reasonable person. She let things go when she didn't have the time to do them right. She bathed Sparky only once every month or two and brushed him once in a while to get out the knots and keep the shedding down. Her mother disapproved and would try to bathe Sparky when she wasn't home, but Sparky made it very difficult.

Helen was very excited when she found the house. It was in a somewhat industrial neighborhood and quite near a freeway, but it was old and had some charm and was very cheap. As Helen packed up her things and moved from her mother's house at last, she heaved a deep sigh of relief. She would be queen of her new home and she and Sparky could start a new life together. They could do whatever they wanted. They would eat ice cream for breakfast. They would leave dishes on the coffee table overnight if they wanted to. They would play ball in the yard (after she planted some seed since it was mostly dirt now), and they would sit out on their new fresh lawn and read great books and she would have friends over for dinner parties and Sparky would watch people go by when she was at work and it would just be such a wonderful improvement over this past year with her mother. No one would be straightening up her desk, making her bed with the sheets tucked under the mattress, refiling books she was still reading: None of it. It was her turn to have a castle.

The house was old and the people who had just moved out hadn't cleaned up after themselves. They were not given their security deposit back, but the landlord kept the money and told Helen that she had to clean it since the rent was so cheap. Helen didn't care for that arrangement much, but she didn't want to rock the boat since they were just moving in and he had allowed her to have a big dog. Many people renting to pet owners say it's okay if it's a small or even a medium sized dog, but if you have a large dog, well, there's just no disguising his size so you have to say it is definitely not medium in any sense of the word. Most often they don't rent to you if you don't lie. Helen told the truth, and she appreciated that this time the truth was rewarded.

So, Helen set to cleaning the house. She scrubbed and scoured and put in shelf lining and repainted some chipped spots in the walls and on the counters, then she spent several hard days whipping the place into shape. It looked much better. Much better. But somehow it still didn't look clean. She was tired and had to unpack, so she figured she'd work on it here and there when she had time. That first night they were so happy, sleeping in her own room with her own things and she let Sparky sleep on the bed just this once since it was a special occasion. She could do that now, since she was the boss of herself.

Now it happened that Helen got very busy at work during the next few weeks. She had deadlines and lots of pressure and co-workers were even calling her at home, so the place was never properly set up from the beginning. It just got off on a bad foot. It was catch up from the getgo. Perhaps that's a large part of the later problems.

Sparky was feeling somewhat neglected since Helen was working so much and he didn't have her mom for company, such as she was. Helen hadn't had time for the seeding of the lawn and it was soon going to be the rainy season which would be the perfect time to put seed in, but she was awfully busy. Sparky spent a lot of his time sitting in the dirt and subsequently got fleas. Now that he was sleeping in the bed he passed several fleas on to Helen. Helen was not lackadaisical about her assault on the fleas. She bought flea powder and a flea collar and vacuumed twice a day and gave Sparky several baths and then she sat down and was exhausted. She looked around the house and became depressed by the mess. She picked herself back up and did some laundry and washed down a few more walls and washed a few more light fixtures and finally collapsed.

The next day was Sunday and she woke up early. She was going to plant the grass seed. She noticed that there was a fine layer of dirt on the light fixture that she had just washed the night before. She had left it on the kitchen counter to dry and now it was dirty already, in just *one day*. She shrugged it off and had her coffee and spent the day tilling the ground and spreading manure and seed and watering and feeling good about herself. This undertaking was much easier if she put the dirty light fixture completely out of her mind, although she realized something was nagging at her all day. She noticed that the sound of the nearby freeway was very loud when she was in her backyard, and the cars went by on her street too fast. Maybe it is a short cut to somewhere, she surmised.

She went back to work on Monday and was still very busy. She failed to realize that while she worked, Sparky walked and lay and peed on the very area she had just seeded. He was also very attracted to the manure. When she came home that night, Sparky needed a good bath and the yard needed reseeding. Helen went to bed early that night and left the dishes from dinner sitting on the kitchen counter since she was simply too tired.

The ant invasion the next morning nearly put her into a frenzy since she had vowed that when she had her own place she wouldn't be a creature killer as she called her mom (who had every retail toxin available). She left the dishes, hoping the ants would eat everything interesting and go away by the time she came home. Instead, the cockroaches had joined them in a food orgy by that night. She saw them scatter as she turned on the light when she came home late that evening. Sucking it up, she washed all the dishes without even eating and went directly to bed. That morning, the dishes that she had washed the night before were filmy with dirt. She shut the kitchen windows tight in defense and ate a quick breakfast and went directly to work.

At work, she looked stressed and her co-worker asked her if she was okay. She explained the situation and showed the coworker her flea bites that were now red and bleeding from her incessant scratching. She tried to make her friend understand that as soon as she did anything, cleaned anything, it was dirty the next day. When she went to bed, even her skin didn't seem clean. She felt that her efforts were all in vain. Her co-worker told her to snap out of it and call the landlord and exterminate for cockroaches and ants and fleas. She did call, that very day, and the landlord grumbled but agreed to send someone out the next week. She felt relieved and empowered. Things were going to be okay she reasoned. She had her own house, she was making enough money to pay for it and she just had to do more cleaning and stay on top of things. Unhappily, she felt much better, knowing that an exterminator would soon be there.

When she came home, Sparky had scratched himself raw and as he continued, she could see the dirt emanate from him. She tried to ignore this. She pet his head and her hands were gray afterward but she washed them. She also noticed that the drawer liners she had put inside the drawers were peeling already. She slid the kitchen rug over to cover the ripped linoleum. She scratched her ankles. She watched some TV and went to bed. She kicked Sparky off the shaking bed when he started scratching.

When the weekend came, she cleaned like a woman possessed. She replanted the grass seed and roped it off. She was determined to triumph. On Monday it started to rain. Sparky now had nowhere to go to the bathroom and lay in his own poop until it got wet and the now comingled rain and crud cocktail ran downhill into his doghouse. Sparky got another bath that night too.

The kitchen cabinets didn't close completely and the floating filth of her neighborhood that so easily found its way inside her house just stuck to her dishes as readily as everything else. So, naturally, the dishes inside the cabinets were dirty whenever she went to use them. She hated to admit it, really hated it, but she missed living in her mother's house. In retrospect, comparatively, it was effortless to clean. When it was cleaned, it stayed that way for a week or longer. She had hated her mother's vigilance, her compulsion, but now she longed for those qualities, and she longed for the satisfaction they could bring.

One night, Helen noticed that the same chipped dish was always dirty and she was always washing it. She wondered how many times she had washed that same dish in her life since she remembered it from her mother's house and had washed it many times there. In order to squelch these dead-end thoughts she did something crazy; she threw the chipped dish in the garbage. She didn't need to be reminded every bloody day that her life was a series of useless, meaningless routines. Washing the dishes that night, she chipped another as it slipped from her hand and crashed into the sink. Her eyes teared up. 'What's happening to me?' She asked, hoping someone with a higher understanding was listening.

She noticed that she now had flea bites around her stomach. She rewashed Sparky with the flea dip and he seemed sick and listless afterward and she realized that it was the kind of flea medicine that you are supposed to wash off immediately but she had thought that you leave it on for twenty-four hours like the last kind. Sparky was poisoned, Helen was devastated, but a few days later, his energy started to return. She gave him lots of water and fresh vegetables and boiled chicken. She put him in the bathtub and rubbed him down hard to remove the toxins from his skin. Then the exterminator came. Sparky was allergic to the spray that was used and had to be rushed to the emergency room. His immune system was now compromised and he could no longer live in the uncleanable house with Helen. Helen's mother had to take him back and he lived out his days in the suburbs in her immaculate house and was thoroughly, forcefully bathed once a week. Regardless of these efforts, he never returned to his full vim and vigor.

'It's only clean for a day,' Helen found herself repeating to herself. 'Clean for one day'. She missed Sparky and that made her depressed. She hoped she could move as soon as her lease was up to a place that was cleaner and neater and newer where she and Sparky could live together again. She looked forward to that. Cockroaches eventually returned and the bug spray she had no longer worked. It could poison a dog but not a cockroach, she shuddered. She had nightmares of ants crawling over her and then they really were when she woke up. She started to clean in the morning before work and then when she came home from work, but it never seemed to be enough. She washed her hands more and more often. She didn't want to have anyone come over because she thought the house would never be acceptable. The winter rains made the roof leak and water dribbled down the wall and peeled back the paint and soon she had bright orange rorschachian mold that could almost pass for wallpaper. She called the landlord and he said that she was getting to be a problem and that she should just scrub it with bleach and stop calling him. She did, but the mold didn't seem to fear bleach. She now had an allergic response to the mold and was stuffy and sneezy and had difficulty breathing. She went to visit Sparky and he seemed depressed too and she blamed herself. He was still scratching, but now the vet said it was just a nasty habit. She went home and scrubbed some more and then something that had been wound very tightly within her snapped and she just gave out.

Her sheets are crisp and white now and smell of bleach. The softly soothing pale pink walls are scrubbed down weekly. People check on her many times a day. She has her own room, but little privacy. She goes to daily counseling sessions downstairs, although the common area is still off-limits to her after her recent outburst.

They found her on the floor, with a three-day layer of dirt on her body. Even though she now lives in a nearly sterile environment she washes her hands until they bleed and scratches her legs where there are no bites and she plays ball with an invisible dog and repeatedly mutters a little jingle to herself that she made up: 'Clean for a day, I'm clean for a day, it's only clean for a day.'

Imaginary Friends

My name is Jacques and I'm an imaginary friend. I'll be narrating this story because the human to whom I am an imaginary friend is so out-to-lunch that he could not narrate a tooth brushing. That's where we come in. He has no real friends. He even has pretty lame imaginary friends. Some imagination! But then I've heard that some people don't have imaginary friends at all, so having lame ones shows more imagination than *that*.

This human, his name is Herb, well, he's a Herb. He's pretty unlikable and never seems to know what to say in most situations and certainly doesn't know what to do. We have to help, each in our own way and skill level. There are, let's see, six of us. You'll meet them, so I'm not going to do the full round of introductions, because you know how that goes, I'll forget their names and be embarrassed and you'll never remember them anyway, so, what's the point of making myself sweat? So, Herb is out of work again and looking for a job, admittedly a demeaning and pathetic time in anyone's life, but he is just not rising to the challenge. We are all committed to the (Lost) Cause of Herb and doing our best, but we're not geniuses. I mean, if we were, we would be imaginary friends of a much better class of person.

Herb has sent out so many resumes and answered so many blind ads that he has now started to lose hope. Basically, he has taken to sitting around and watching a lot of TV. Can I tell you how much I hate watching TV? I check out at the first sign of that universal remote control and relinquish the next round of hand-holding to Angie. She seems to enjoy and actually understand the shows and even the commercials, but she's seven, so she has a distinct advantage. I pride myself on finding them obtuse.

We are all worried about Herb's mental state at the moment since he is obviously depressed and thinking dark thoughts. We got together last night while he was sleeping and considered an intervention. But Rebel thinks it's premature, especially since interventions have become mainstream and he hates all things mainstream, but also he thinks that maybe it could be good for Herb somehow to connect to his dark side, so we decided to wait and see if anything improves. We'll give him a week and then it's off to the shrink for some uppers. Who wants to be around a depressive all the time, and I mean all the time? We all agreed we'd prefer Venlafaxine, so we'll advocate for that when the time comes.

Herb normally works as an auditor, yes, thank you for the empathy. When his company was indicted in one of those massive covered-up-then-overexposed scandals, Herb was one of the first to be cut. He was uninvolved, although that's mostly because he was out of the gravy train loop since he never socialized, but regardless, no one wanted to hire anyone from that company and every employee was suspect. Herb now feels like he's under an undeserved cloud. A lot of his fellow former employees have found work again, but Herb refuses to lie on his resume as they did. So he remains out of a job, watching *Friends* on TV and wondering why he's being punished. It gets old. So, as I said, we are giving him one short week more of this moping before we cry a collective 'Uncle'.

Herb's mother is coming over today. She is a case too. She thinks in the back of her mind that Herb is slightly mentally deficient. She blames his father, naturally. She sees him a bit as, perhaps not an *idiot* savant, but perhaps a *slow* savant. He's good with numbers, she acknowledges, always was, which she sees as a true sign of his savantism, but the rest of the package never developed properly. She knew about us, way back when, but Herb has convinced her that he has outgrown 'the voices'. It's better that way. She finds no fault in herself as she did all she could. She was normal, after all. Since Herb's late father can no longer defend himself, although we don't believe he ever really gave it much of a college try, he is usually the culprit in these matters.

She is coming to give Herb a check to tide him over against her better judgment, and to try to 'cheer him up'. Herb is dreading her visit, but needs the money. For an auditor, he is not very good with his own money. He doesn't spend it on anything ostentatious or something that you would even notice, but he never gets ahead. Julia thinks he's seeing prostitutes since if he ever gets sexual she immediately bolts so she would never know. But the rest of us just think he buys too many meals out and too many mocha javas and too many white shirts and is too timid to ask for raises. So, Herb has had to mentally get himself up for his mother's coming by talking incessantly to himself in the mirror and asking our honest opinion of these minor untruths and then desperately, pitifully seeking our approval. The sycophants and the wimps among us fill that role, but the rest of us tell him to pick up his balls from the floor and tuck them back where they belong. He will occasionally respond to that kind of rough talk.

Herb's mother lets herself in with her own key. Herb gave it to her like a fool when she asked after handing over a check so he felt like he couldn't refuse.

"Yoohoo, Herbie," she shouts and the hair on our collective neck rises. Herb kisses her on the cheek and in her presence immediately becomes even more of a weakling than usual.

"So, Herbie, I have a job lead for you. You know your successful cousin Henry who runs the dry cleaning company? Well, he says he needs some help with the business books and he could use your 'expertise,' that's what he called it. I brought his number so you could call him right away."

"Dry cleaning? I really don't know ..."

"I know." Herb's mother always knows. "Do you want the money this week or not? Because if you don't promise to call tomorrow, no check."

Herb grovels and promises to call. They go out to dinner, her treat, and I decide that I need to have some peace and quiet and stay home. It's an occasional indulgence. I drank a beer and read an Elmore Leonard novel, thoroughly enjoying my solitude, so I can't report on their evening, but Julia told me that it was hard to watch. Herb's mother is a real ball-buster and Herb is so downtrodden these days that most of us don't have the stomach for her visits. Rebel's usually the one to accompany him on these occasions. Julia said at one point Herb started to cry and his mother gave him a handkerchief. We shook our heads in disgust. She said that Rebel gave Herb an earful on the way home and Herb kept losing his train of thought with his mother because of this, and at one point he told Rebel to shut up and his mother slapped him. All the work we did was really a waste of time I thought. How unsatisfying. I am Sisyphus, I lamented.

Now, Dog is Herb's best friend. He is the one Herb most favors, and Dog is the most trusted among us. Dog is extremely loyal to Herb and never criticizes him and is basically more of a pussycat if you ask me, which is part of Herb's problem. He doesn't need yes-men. He needs cojones. But anyway, when he goes on walks, or short, non-confrontational errands, Dog always goes along. And then at night, Dog fills us in. But Dog's assessment of Herb is always so syrupy positive, and we all know that's bull, so we try to trick-question the truth out of him. Since he refuses to spill the beans, we have to imagine the rest.

Herb has started to frequent this fast-food Chinese restaurant down the street and has taken to going there when he's just received a check from his mother and acting like a big shot to the waitress.

"Is she cute?" we all ask Dog, and he says oh yes, so we figure she's just okay. Like I said, you have to take everything from Dog with a grain of salt.

Herb asks to speak to her if she isn't at the counter (he knows her nights off), so she comes out from the back, and he asks for extra soy sauce or something stupid and smiles and, eventually she got the idea. So, this last time, he actually got up the courage to ask her out on a date and shockingly she said she would go.

Now if there's any dating to be done, which there usually isn't, I'm the one that goes along. The females are useless and would ruin everything, Rebel's a hothead and Boy is, well, three, and Dog is a damn dog. I'm the only one with this kind of experience and expertise and finesse. But then I find out he has asked her to go bowling. This is not my best milieu. This is not what I would have suggested, but Dog didn't have any ideas and it was the first thing Herb thought of. I like a challenge, but Herb can't bowl and it's so damn loud in those places there's little opportunity for dialog, and nobody looks cool bowling. You have those dorky shoes and you have to contort your body and have I said, he can't bowl? Did he think she looked like a bowler? Did she ever mention her burning desire to bowl? What could have possessed him?

When I ask, informing him that we are going to have to do some fancy footwork to salvage the evening, he says that it will keep them occupied so that she won't realize that he has very little to say. He has a point. Did he call his successful cousin? Julia interrupts, wanting to know. Herb acknowledges he will before the date, so he can tell her he has some prospects without bald-faced lying.

His cousin says he can come in to talk to him that week, so Herb is the picture of overconfidence the night of the date. I tell him to take it easy, Valentino. We decide he should wear an actual bowling shirt that was his father's to seem playful and some plain black jeans. He looks acceptable.

We pick her up at her house around 7:30 (why didn't you ask

her out to dinner, I wonder, and he says that he wasn't sure he could afford it, so he told her to eat before he got there). I am not expecting much because of this kind of tolerance on her part, but she isn't actually too bad. Plain but kind of charming in her own way. These are the kinds of things you come to appreciate when you pass forty, which makes me so valuable.

So, I tell him to be cool and open her car door and ask her how her day was and act interested and to ask if she knows how to bowl and let her know right off the bat that he sucks so she doesn't expect to learn anything. They seem to be doing okay so I kind of check out during the actual bowling, which is pretty routine. You watch the other person, check the scores, get a round of drinks, clap when they hit something and look upset for them if the ball goes in the gutter. There are a lot of those fake sad looks since neither one of them had any technique or skill. I tell him to tell her she's cute and that he has been coming into the restaurant because he wanted to get to know her, but he says 'thanks for coming out with me,' which to him is pretty risqué and takes a lot of courage, so I let it go. He touches her hand when he reaches for his drink, and I tell him that is very smooth and he mentions it for days afterward.

So, they go for an ice cream sundae afterward, which I think is way too retro and unhip, but he feels that that's the kind of girl she is, and I'm sort of surprised that he overrode my idea of going to hear some jazz which is quite ballsy of him. After the sundae, which seems to go over fairly well, he does suggest the jazz, but she says she has to work the next morning and her mother expects her. Okay, she has to be thirty-five and this sets off all kinds of red flags for me, but Herb is smitten and says of course and starts the car.

I tell him to reach for her hand, ask her when he can see her again and tell her that he had a great time—one of the above. He says nothing and asks which way to turn on Pickwick. He stops the car at her house and she starts to open the door. I am screaming now, tell her something, try to kiss her, and he says only that he enjoyed their evening and hopes that she will agree to see him again. She actually says that she will and gives him her number and says if her mother answers, hang up. She then leans in and kisses him on the cheek and says thank you for asking. This evening is full of surprises I think.

For the next few days all we hear about is the date and how well he did for himself (what an ego!) and that he was going to have a job soon and things were right again. We forget about the intervention, but discuss that this is nearly as bad as depression, this inflated sense of self and embarrassing lack of perspective. But at least this is something we can ridicule, and depression is sort of off-limits.

Anyway, he calls her and sets up another date and this time he said he wants to go by himself or maybe just take Dog. I am hurt, of course, but even more, I am concerned for him. He is certainly not ready to go it alone after one minor success. He says that he feels ready and needs to start testing himself and trusting his own ideas and words.

"Why?" I want to know: "Why now?"

"I'm not getting any younger" is all he has to say for himself.

I warn him about my other concerns with regard to her ties to mama and that she still lives at home and she was awfully eager to kiss his cheek which is not a good sign, but he just ignores my advice and asks to speak to Dog.

Well, that night we all have a discussion and I say that this is not good, this reliance upon Dog's advice, no offense intended, but come on! Even Dog agrees, but I say that if Herb is deciding to disregard us and our wisdom, well that is a real bad long-term job sign. Julia and I talk about new psychological ways to undermine him so that he will need us to straighten it all out (we call it insecurity security), and Boy, who has never, ever, uttered a word listens and Angie talks about whatever pops into her mind, usually a jingle or a slogan, and Rebel says he agrees with Herb's intuition to go it alone. We all stare at Rebel but he says he will surely get a better assignment when this one ends and he attributes Herb's rebellion against us as a direct tribute to all the work he had done to teach Herb to see the anarchist perspective and that if we weren't so selfish and jealous and loaded with puss that we would be able to see it too. Well, we go to bed angry that night, even though they tell us never to do that.

Julia and I try to work on him to at least Google this girl and consider that the living at home thing is going to be an issue in the future, and we try to tell him to invite her to a play or something to discover her views on art and politics, but he has already invited her to see a Disney film. We groan en masse and then he does something extraordinary—He turns on the TV. Angie tries to push past us to join him, but we decide to stick it out even though it is torturous because we feel it is for his own good, but he turns the volume up really loud and Angie runs between our legs so we just give up and go back and have a stiff drink.

Now the rest is a bit hazy, because I ended up getting pretty drunk, but somehow Boy ended up sitting up with Herb until late at night (way past his bedtime which shows what's wrong with kids these days—I guess he had lousy parents—but that's just no excuse for what happened). Anyway, Boy talked! He turned on us and talked. It is a shock to all of us and we've learned a valuable lesson not to let kids in on adult discussions and to explain in no uncertain terms what a secret is. We've also learned to keep our big stupid mouths shut in mixed company.

So, they stayed up talking and Herb expressed his doubts about our advice regarding this woman he was interested in, and said that he felt that we were often too harsh with him and that we were mean to his mother and then Boy says, "I think it's a secret, but Julia and Jacques and all the rest of them try to keep you from trusting yourself. But they're only parts of yourself that you have given up control of because you don't trust yourself. So you could just ignore them and they would go away."

"You mean they don't really exist?"

"We're like Santa Claus. We only exist as long as you believe that we do."

Herb considered Boy. What could he really know, since he was three? And since when did three year-olds not believe in Santa Claus? Yet somehow it sounded plausible. Herb thought about what each of us gave him and he couldn't find much there.

He felt foolish that he hadn't figured this out before and it had taken Boy to make him come to his senses. He thought he'd have more luck with girls without Julia, who was really more of a mother figure, and more confidence without me since with me there he could be lazy, and more good sense without Rebel who got him into verbal conflicts with strangers, and he could watch TV with his new girlfriend so he wouldn't need Angie, and he started to think for himself for real. He wondered if just keeping an imaginary dog best friend could be very harmful, and made a bold decision.

The danger warning signs were flashing in my brain. What had that retarded Boy done? We had never felt compelled to tell him to keep quiet because he never spoke at all. He was so freakin' damaged who would have thought he would be able to put two sentences together anyway? And then he is our undoing, like some judas. That's what we get for leaving the back door open.

I felt lightning bolts in my head. I sensed a gigantic tide of tumult arising deep within me and felt intensely nauseous. And then, like a mere blip on the screen, they all at once ceased to exist in any real or imaginary way, except Dog, who lived an exceptionally long life for a dog although I never mentioned him to anyone, not even my new wife from the Chinese restaurant and her mother who lived with us until she died at age ninety-one.

Industryland

You smell it before you see it. Industryland stands like a sooty, stained, belching monument to exactly what it was: capitalism at its finest. At the expense of the environment, of course. But ironically, that's why it exists at all.

Gary, Indiana. What other wasteland could you leave entirely untended to become, in negligence, Industryland? As you can imagine, it was a lucrative contract, so there were several contenders. It was all decided by another 5-to-4 decision by the U.S. Supreme Court. Even though Detroit really let itself go in anticipation of getting the contract, the Michigan city still had some civic pride since the Pistons kept winning basketball games and even though their fan base had greatly eroded, it just never went as downhill as Gary because of the team. Gary had no such entanglements. First it was white flight, then black flight, then Hispanic flight, finally, rat flight—I believe some undeterred cockroaches were the last holdouts. It was virtually abandoned, which was perfect for the purpose (otherwise they would have had to buy people off the land, which could have eventually added up to something). In this ideal, undiluted, toxic state, Disney didn't have to build Industryland from scratch. It was exactly what they were going for anyway, and it was *real*; it had to be approved by the board of directors however, since that isn't the way Disney usually does things, authentically. Despite reservations, the board bought it: *The Dirtiest Place on Earth*. And that's a tall order.

It all came about through a seemingly random, yet somehow foreseeable grand plan, somewhat like evolution but much less noble. Republicans began having more kids due to the economic upturn for them alone. It seems that the top five percent economically was 93% republican, so they just kept pressing Congress to pass tax laws that continued to benefit them and, voila, no one else made any money. Their per capita child birth rate approached that of immigrants for a time—trophy wives had to sign pre-nups that mandated children. After Michael Moore's documentary *Fahrenheit 9/11* in the early 21st century, more republicans joined the Disney bandwagon since it was Disney that initially refused to distribute the film, fearful that their theme park tax burdens would be adversely affected, and with that came the letters. First, the nasty, pleading, demanding, threatening letters—these were ignored. But after some think tank scuttlebutt, letters began arriving explaining that rich people would love to invest in Disney stock, and they had lots to invest they assured the board, but there was a catch. There always is. But this one came as a carrot rather than a stick. Wait, I'm getting ahead of myself.

First, we had to come thisclose to destroying everything. With corporate profits growing at such an extremely accelerated pace for so long, and a large new crop of offspring not doing much but expecting a pile of cash for it, a lot of people willingly lost sight of the actual costs of those profits. How much things really should have cost when you take in the superfund clean-up sites and the natural resources destroyed (no more camping trips to the natural world), and the loss of human jobs replaced by technology and robots which were created using more and more resources, and the disposal of toxins in communities which caused a lot of class action law suits whose burdens were passed on to the consumers along with the health care costs that no one could afford any longer since the very air we breathed and water we drank was killing us all, and the loss of habitat for animals and plants which led to mass extinctions of which some of those plants could have provided disease cures and the collapse of complete ecosystems so that all that survived were noxious weeds for hundreds of square miles. We saved some of the important stuff since not everyone had his eyes shut, but we lost a lot too. Thus began a real renaissance in zoos, which until then had been outlawed as cruel, but ironically, became sanctuaries. After all, most humans at that time were basically living on handouts and in cages too. Zoos created hope somehow and people flocked to them.

As you can imagine, this all led to a lot of hatred toward industry and capitalism for the exploitation and desecration of our world. As in every movement, there is the inevitable countermovement. And the pendulum nearly broke as it swung back (think crack the whip). The entire gross national product was mandated to be reinvested in the planet. The air was purified through great carbon intake filters; the water was beset upon by oil-and-bacteria-and-filth-eating microbes; oil for industry was made at vast factories out of used tires and wallpaper and disposable diapers; fuel efficiency in vehicles reached 125 miles per gallon; landfills were pressurized by extremely massive equipment and the resulting solid mass was used as armor for the walls of the President's and Congress's and former leaders' of industry homes to prevent mortar attacks by the citizens; the recycling program became an activist movement and there were outings of non-recyclers—found by police assigned to garbage detail—and homes were spray-painted with words like *Evildoer* and *Outcast*; eating or wearing any animal product was strictly forbidden, punishable by a very stiff prison term, and since this was a particularly heinous crime, these offenders were treated like child molesters in prison by the other, higher-minded prisoners;

anyone coming to your door asking for help was required to be given a meal, cash and a clean set of clothes and it was *really* illegal not to open the door; holistic health care was fully embraced once again—are you sensing the cyclic nature of all things yet?—and the costs of health care plummeted since people were eating and breathing better and had clean water to drink. Hemp became the national flower. It was finally publicly acknowledged that the school system had been purposely neglected so that the poor had no chance to improve. This tacitly accepted caste system had provided everyone else with a steady supply of laborers (educated people wouldn't do those jobs for that pay) and soldiers (educated people began hiring others to do their killing long ago) and prisoners (upon whom to pin our crimes and necessary fears, as well as fodder for our prison system, that all important constituent industry especially in poor, depressed towns—a reverse NIMBY thing) but mainly to have some group to blame for our failures. Someone had to be bringing us down other than ourselves, since the rich could easily buy their way, through courts of course, out of any criminal act. The problem for them is that the fall guys finally started to vote, which ignited the subsequent revolution. That's the thing with humans, you can push them for a long time, and you can push them pretty far, but eventually they push back. And by the time the pushing becomes shoving, there are more than enough people on the bottom to topple the pyramid.

But there's always the nostalgicites who miss what's gone no matter what it is; in this case, the industrial revolution and its soot and its corporate heyday. It made them nouveau riche after all. But since it had all been relatively cleaned up, someone had to champion the opposite. If we hadn't had the Socioenvironmental Revolution, we wouldn't have Industryland at all. Everything has a backlash as they say. Long ago, at the beginning of the mass destruction, they created national parks as somewhere for tree huggers to go. Now, they created Industryland for the republicans to reminisce, cry in their martinis, commiserate with like-minded narrow-minds, rekindle the furnace of molten lead within, be somebody again in this mausoleum of a museum and not feel like an anachronism. This was all late in the 21st century. It took a while, as the big ideas usually do. The church donations, the corporate venture-capitalist backers, the hedge fund managers' solicitations to clients, the money saved on estate taxes, the discreet collection boxes at all Hilton hotel front desks, the Christian coalition internet pleas, it all added up. That demand and its cash bodyguard eventually incubated Industryland.

Enough with American History 101. I'm H.L. Shunkenflecken, writer for the *Good Times* and I've decided to take the tour. I'm not what you would call a republican nor a capitalism lover. I'm a journalist born after all the hubbub occurred and want to know what the whole thing was about. We don't have any exposed filthy vestiges of this bygone era anymore. I guess some people miss it, because the lines to get in to Industryland can set you back hours you'll never have again. All of the 'Manufacturing' jobs went to various third world countries many years before. Now, we consider ourselves 'Service Seulement'. What must that whole time have been like? Was it so innocent, regulation-free, cowboys-and-Indians as it was portrayed? And I figured it was better than another weekend at DisneyUniverse with the kids.

As I stood in line, I was looking forward to it all: crime re-enactments; black lung machines in action; The Museum of Cancer (still statistically significant in Gary—that's why the wages and health benefits are so outstanding—it will remain toxic for several hundred more half lives, so most visitors opt for the $50 gas mask rental); tenement slums; cafés that were called fast food joints that serve cheap food of bad quality; the company store that includes ledgers with the amounts owed by employees that always added up to more than the person made in wages—this always brings a tear to the eye; a dated independent chemical analysis of the various kinds of toxins in the air and water and ground of various cities, unearthed from the archives of the self-policing Industry Fund (it turns out it wasn't *that* polluted after all!); a fashion show of the workers' uniforms actually worn; a tour of the local clinic with re-enactments of humans slicing into each other with sharp, shiny tools and a hair salon with something called 'permanents' and much more!

As a journalist, one area where I really want to spend some time is The Kenneth Lay Memorial Library containing all the evidence, the documents, the testaments to a bygone time. Before corporations were forced to give it all up, they had quite a time of it. No responsibilities, no taxes, no fears from regulators, nothing they couldn't handle. Mining rights for five cents an acre that they could build condos on when they were done defacing; Enron-style accounting that was so complicated the auditors threw up their hands, signing off on the whole putrid mess; trials where the jurors were either bought or threatened into compliance; trial judges bribed or better still, appointed by politicians you had bribed (they even had a name for it—human laundering); tax credits for non-existent workers; plenty of loopholes to keep the lawyers busy. It was the best of times. It was a national frontier town and a free-for-all, and in some ways, you can understand the romanticism. However, it blew up in all of our faces, as rampant graft usually does. It cost every man, woman, child and fetus over 50,000 dollars. Most of the working people didn't make nearly that much. It caused the mother of all deficits. Heads rolled. Things changed. Somehow, Life went on. And now, here we are at Industryland. It takes a village, well, a well-heeled community anyway, to raise an incubus.

My wife didn't want to come. She said she wouldn't support what it stood for and pay $500 for the privilege. But I'm more than willing to pay $500 to visit Industryland. As I pull out my wallet, I smile, grateful for its existence, happy to be here. Grateful for its containment in Gary, Indiana, USA. Grateful that at the end of the day's tours, they can turn off the lights and shut it down. If the capitalists had won this war I'd be paying $1,000,000 right now to visit Earth.

Beauty Isn't Pretty

"Would you like to try our new fragrance … Dew Drop? If you buy the larger eau de cologne size this month, you will receive our free spring gift collection."

The passerby allowed the perfume to be sprayed upon her wrist, but declined the purchase and free gift.

It takes a great deal of training to become an Estee Lauder beauty product sales person at Nordstrom's. And this was an upscale mall, so it was an even more prestigious and difficult position to attain. The plated gold nametag with the black letters that spells 'Joy', her name as well as what she is selling, alerts the shopper that she knows beauty products. The classic lines of her face, the polished skin and perfect makeup application and the jaunty curl of her hair, still perky at the end of the day, shows that she knows beauty itself.

Her smile is also perfected. It shows just enough of her whiteness-enhanced teeth. It is aloof and cool, yet knowing and inviting. Buy something from me and you may attain this smile yourself. These products may well give you the confidence to smile this way also. Because I know what I am doing for a good reason. I have spent years at this counter because it's important. Our mutual commitment to looking our best is important. This look is worth it. You're worth it. Let me show you what's new in beauty and perhaps it will change your life. Today could be the day that you look in the mirror and see the beauty you always knew you really were because we have created this product just for you. My smile, my presence here, lets you know that this is a damn important job. With these looks, I could be in Hollywood or on the cover of some glossy fashion mag, but I chose to spend my working life valuing others and their pursuit of the perfect look. Don't tell me that you aren't interested. I know you are. Years ago, when I merely shopped here, I saw the woman who had this job and I wanted to be her. And now I know that others look at me that way. Don't think I don't feel the pressure of those stares. It's a lot to live up to. But I'm not hawking products, I'm reinventing you. Come on, don't wander over to Lancome. The Estee Lauder look is over here.

There is a lot behind that smile.

Joy was tired. Her jaw hurt from smiling today. It was one of those days. She had them, just like everyone else, but you wouldn't know it by looking at her. She had reapplied her foundation at lunch knowing that it was going to be one of those days and she needed a little something extra. Her commissions depended upon her looking fresh, not lockjawed and irritable and stale. And she didn't do so well today. It was subtle. She looked fine, but not spot on. It never failed. The cash register told the real truth. She needed to get a good night's rest. She needed to be dew drop fresh tomorrow. She had a car payment due next week.

She discreetly checked her watch. Thirty-five minutes to go. She pouted slightly, then went back to her counter and rearranged some of the products under the glass counter. The beige bisque had nearly commingled with the belle bisque. That's how horrible mistakes happened. She was glad she had checked. She sprayed some of the

Dew Drop perfume in the air above her and waited for it to mist down toward her nose. It *was* pretty, she decided. She hadn't really liked it much when she first smelled it, but she knew that during the month of being exposed to it, she had better learn to like it or it would be an awfully long month. So she did. She was like that. Feminine but practical at the same time.

In a very hushed and respectful tone the automated speaker voice announced that the store would be closing in ten minutes and shoppers should make their final selections. An out of breath woman hurried over to Joy's counter and said she needed some emergency lipstick advice as she had an important event that night and wasn't sure what to wear with her dress. She had brought the dress to work and now to the store so she could be sure. Joy respected that kind of diligence. She spent her last ten minutes with this woman exclusively, helping her choose. Joy wished she had had more time with the woman as she could have given her some other pointers as well, but you do what you can where you can. The woman gratefully thanked Joy for all the help. "You're a lifesaver," she said as she paid and left. Joy smiled. All in a day's work.

She drove her six month-old Acura Legend the .08 miles back to her apartment. She would never walk to work in the heels she wore all day. And only soccer moms bring their tennis shoes to work. Besides, parking was included in her pay package so she wanted to make sure she got the full measure of her benefits. She was already getting varicose veins she feared (she noticed them one night when she was waxing the back of her thighs and had to bring out a makeup mirror with all the bulbs on to determine what she was really looking at and sure enough, veins) so she had taken to lying down as much as possible when she got home from work. She had also bought some vein crème from a competitor (Estee Lauder didn't carry such products as the Estee Lauder ideal didn't need them). But she didn't want to take any chances. She had written a note to Ms. Lauder personally about the need for such extraneous beauty aids however unpretty they were to discuss, along with her personal recommendations for various products under a new, practical offshoot line. She was waiting for a reply. It was something she had going on the back burner.

She kicked her shoes off and took a celery stick from the fridge. She looked through her mail: bills mostly, but also her new Cosmo had arrived. She went over to the couch to read it, propping up her feet. Sure enough, Liz Hurley was on the cover. She had heard that she was going to be, but was excited to see that it was true anyway. Joy had really pulled for Liz to get the 'Face' of Estee Lauder contract. Like Joy, Liz had the perfect 1.618 to 1 ratio throughout her face. Joy knew because she had measured herself and various pictures of Liz. Everyone in the know knew that this was the essence of true beauty—the correct ratio—not anything you could buy. Either you had it or you didn't. Of course Joy never shared this secret information with her clients. Hope did not dwell in numbers, but in products. Joy had the sneaking suspicion that Liz and many other perfects had had some work done. Joy was really proud that she was all natural. However, she didn't rule out the possibility that in the future she might need a little help.

She didn't notice her message light was blinking as she finished the celery stick. As her eyes closed, she wished she could just lie there, fall asleep and forget about all she had to do that night. She almost did fall asleep, but caught herself and shook herself awake. Not tonight. That car payment loomed.

She reached for the varicose vein crème that she kept secreted in a covered container on her coffee table and began to rub it into her thighs. Her stomach growled as she leaned forward. She ignored its request.

She had wanted the expensive car that said success in most businesses. She told herself that after ten years with Nordstrom's and Estee Lauder that she would buy herself the car she should be driving. She hadn't really saved as much as she had hoped when the time came, but she had made a promise to herself and a promise made is a debt unpaid. Besides it wasn't just the car that had put her behind. It was the little things. All the little extras that she needed, but didn't really budget for. Her makeup, the hair products, the best shoes (she was on her feet all day after all), her hose, accessories, all of it. It was part of the package that she was presenting and she could not neglect any one of those things if she wanted to be tops in her field. Someone else would come along that did not neglect these things and undermine her very livelihood. She was too smart for that!

Plus it took the look of money to attract money. She didn't want to end up with some department manager (and there were plenty of those to choose from) if she could attract an entrepreneur or a stockbroker. The only problem with her job is that the attractive, successful men that she met at work were shopping for their wives and girlfriends. Girlfriends weren't that big of an obstacle, but she refused to be a home-wrecker so she always asked for whom the gift was intended and then turned on the charm if the man said his girlfriend. She was very professional all the way if he was a husband. But truthfully, most of her customers were women.

She got up from the couch. Time to get busy. She removed her work clothes and hung them on the hanger by the bathroom door. She exchanged them for a pink cotton robe. She went into the cabinet under the bathroom sink and began to remove products and arrange them on the counter: hair highlighter, a hot wax kit, nail polish remover, a set of manicured nails, clay mask in a jar, a tweezer, a tube of facial hair lightener, curlers, a razor, a cuticle cutter, an egg timer and an emery board.

And she was no barfly. The class of people in those places was deplorable. She had occasional dates and a fix-up here and there, but she was truthfully too busy to have a boyfriend.

She applied the hair lightener to her mustache which was quite visible as she placed her face inches from her lighted mirror. She was expert at the application. She set the egg timer for two minutes. She plugged in the hot wax machine and added the correct amount of wax for only her arms. She wasn't feeling overly ambitious tonight to do the whole body. Anyway, she'd decided she was wearing slacks tomorrow, so she could skip the lower extremities.

Another problem with her job was that there wasn't a great

deal of advancement potential. She already was the manager of the Estee Lauder counter, which took several years of her ten-year stint to attain. Oh, she could go the corporate route, but that just didn't appeal to her. She liked the excitement of the counter and the new faces every day. She knew she would figure it out. She had time. She was only twenty-eight after all.

The timer went off. She removed the hair lightener with a cotton pad and rinsed the area carefully. She applied the clay mask after patting her skin with a hot towel for several minutes to open the pores. She used a clean cotton ball to remove the clear polish currently on her nails. She began to file her nails as she looked at herself in the mirror. The mask was made from bright green clay, but dried to a grayish green, flaky and hard, like the bottom of a dried up river bed she thought as she traced the lines with her finger. She had a brief thought about what her skin might look like one day, when she was old—if these lines in the clay might be real lines on her face. She shook it off as she usually did when thoughts like this occurred. She'd get a lift, she allowed.

She removed the mask with a fresh hand towel and again patted her skin dry. She applied a toning and freshening tonic, then night recovery cream, making her skin glowing and shiny. She pulled a plastic hair cover over her head and began to pull tiny strands of hair through the little holes with a crochet hook. Sometimes she winced as this but she wasn't a flincher. She mixed and shook the hair products and glanced once at the directions just to make sure. She began to apply the white paste with a small brush that was provided with the package.

Most of her friends had boyfriends so it was hard to go out with them alone, especially on weekends. Before they had boyfriends, they all used to go out on Saturday nights to art openings or to fancy hotel bars or to see a show. None of her friends met their boyfriends at those places, however. Most of them met at work. She didn't ask them to fix her up with their boyfriends' friends since most of the boyfriends were not very established nor terribly interesting to her. She was looking for a man, and these were mostly boys.

The timer went off again. She put her head under the faucet and rinsed off the hair paste. She then washed her hair and conditioned it, lastly applying a setting gel. She then blew it semi-dry. She checked her watch and frowned. She still had to apply the nails. She wrapped the damp hair in large rollers. Then she pulled a shapeless cotton cap over her whole head. She looked at herself in the mirror. Like a bloated alien, she thought. She adjusted one of the rollers that was pinching.

Her mother wanted her to get married. She said with Joy's looks, she could have anybody but that looks wouldn't last forever and the clock was ticking. Her mother didn't look so good any longer, although from pictures Joy had seen she had once been quite a beauty. Joy knew her mother was right, that eventually her looks would start to decline. She knew that this beauty ritual she performed every few weeks had taken on more urgency, and seemed to be required more than elective. She knew that she kept buying more and more products to do the same things one or two items used to do. She also knew that she took much better care of herself than her mother had and that she had never smoked and she never went out without sunscreen. She wasn't worried. She was only twenty-eight.

She finished pushing back her cuticles. She trimmed them carefully, not wanting to cut into the quick and bleed. It just burned more when the glue was applied. Oh, she remembered, she needed to pluck her eyebrows before the nails were applied. Once more, she sat inches from the mirror and made the arch of her brow clean. A few stray hairs can ruin the line, she knew. While she was so close she noticed a few pimples. She squeezed them, relieved after a closer examination that they were an aberration. She then began to apply the nails. Most people go to professionals for this, she thought. It had become too expensive, so she had learned to do it herself, like everything else. She did a better job anyway, she reasoned, since no one else could possibly know or care about her body as she did.

When she finally finished with the nails it was eleven o'clock. Luckily she didn't start until ten on Saturdays. Carefully, so as not to disturb the curlers, she removed her robe and pulled an oversized t-shirt over her head. It was stretched so much from regular use that it fit without much maneuvering. She climbed into bed and set the alarm: 8:30. Nine hours. That should give her that extra beauty rest she needed.

She adjusted the curlers behind her head to make herself as comfortable as is possible lying against hard plastic. She knew this was the price for looking great. Curling irons just burn the hair and the curls never last as long as with these old-fashioned curlers. She had learned all this the hard way. She had learned everything she knew the hard way she reasoned as she drifted off to a plastic-cushioned sleep.

Windows

The Fed Ex guy drove by the house this morning really slow, staring at it. He had nothing to deliver to us, he was just driving by, just looking. I imagined he could see me in the window, watching him through his open passenger side door as he returned the lingering look. Did someone tell them where I lived? Maybe Gus from dispatch said to say hello to me. Maybe he was just looking at the address so he could get his bearings on the street, like I used to do, but it didn't seem like that. It seemed like he cared somehow. It seemed like we, almost like we were waving to each other.

That was early this morning and since then, not much has happened. I don't know why I woke up so early this morning because I usually sleep until ten or eleven, but this morning, I was awake in my bed and I just got up. It was very strange, but it happens sometimes. Maybe the sleeping drugs didn't agree with the anchovy pizza I had last night or maybe I was having a weird dream that now

I couldn't remember. I didn't remember my dreams much anymore, since, well, for nearly a year.

Mom was already gone when I got out of bed even though it was very early for me. She had left her usual note with the usual things in it. She wanted me to have a nice day. She wanted me to call if I needed <u>ANYTHING</u>. The word 'anything' was underlined and in capital letters. She reminded me to take my pills, two reds and a blue with milk for breakfast. She wanted me to eat the leftover spaghetti from two nights ago for lunch and if I felt up to it, the garden could use a little tending. Today it was spaghetti, but she could have exchanged the word spaghetti with any other leftover, and it would be the same note every day. If I felt like it, up to it, I would go out in the garden and see if I could pull a few weeds. It would make her feel good and it wouldn't hurt me much.

She had to go back to work about six months ago. She said we needed the money. She said the doctors' bills and the medication, even with the disability and Medicare and Medicaid, were more than she had in the bank. She said we could sell the house or she had to go out and get a job. And we had to live *somewhere*. Also, she was worried that it would upset my nervous system too much to move now. I really wasn't sure if it would or wouldn't, but the way the living room is set up and the way the couch fits and the angle of the TV is just right here.

She works at the Staples store up the street so she can walk there and often comes home for lunch. She doesn't really like working there, she says the lights are too bright and there's no one her own age and none of the cashiers are too smart, but until she finds something better, it's better than nothing. She sells paper and binders and helps people find aisle number seven, where the paper clips are. I think she's bored working there, she could do better I tell her, but she says at her age and with her lack of real job experience, this was the best she could get. She says if she makes manager and gets better pay, then, it won't be so bad. I hope she becomes the manager and then maybe she could hire me to stock shelves or something. I think maybe I could do that. Maybe a day or two a week at least in a few months, when I get better.

I spend the day watching my favorite soap operas and I wash my face but forget to brush my teeth until Mom comes home and reminds me at lunch. We go out in the garden for the spaghetti lunch together and sit at the plastic furniture. It's dirty and Mom wipes it off with a paper towel while I stand nearby and look up at the bird feeder which is empty.

"I'm going to put some seed in that feeder today!" I exclaim as Mom and I sit down for lunch.

"Well, honey, that would be great. I'm glad you noticed that it is empty. That's great."

We eat our lunch and don't say much else. We see each other a lot, and often don't really have anything new to say. I don't tell her about the Fed Ex guy because it would make her sad. So, other than that, I really don't have anything else to share, as Doctor Mark would say. I don't have anything else to share today.

After she left, I decided to go into the garden again and I tried to remember what I told her I would do. It was important, I remembered, it had something to do with, with ... I should have written it down. I stood out there for a minute, and I did pull several weeds from among the lettuces, since I have learned to tell the difference recently. After that I got tired and frustrated because I couldn't remember what I was supposed to do, so I went back inside and ate some ice cream and turned the TV back on and watched Oprah until I fell asleep. I'm supposed to lie down when I get tired and frustrated, so that I don't get over-excited. I'm sure I was extra tired since I woke up so early anyway.

When I woke up I lay on the couch for a long time with the TV on, but not really watching it. I didn't want to get up but I didn't want to stay there either. I think the drugs do that to me. I don't remember being like this before, but I don't really remember any other way either. Mom says it's okay, because at least I don't want to hurt myself anymore and I don't have those other times when I act crazy, but I don't feel very okay. I don't feel much at all.

There's a computer in my bedroom and Mom says I used to be

a whiz on it. That makes me smile, thinking of myself as a whiz. I remember that I worked in an office with a lot of other people in it, and I had my own desk and I did things with that computer, or maybe it was a different one, with photos and changed their colors and shapes and made them fit in pages with words and other pictures. Now, after I turn it on, I don't remember what to do with it. I stare at the screen for a long time, hoping it will do something like the TV, but after a while I stop looking at it and go do something else. Mom says that she's forgotten lots of things too. That makes me feel better because she's not sick at all.

I got fired from that job after I did some bad things there that I can't remember. They said I threw something out of the window and I think we worked high up in an office. I didn't mean to. I guess I couldn't help it, that's what Doctor Mark says. He says I was sick. He says I can get better. That's why we go to see him so often, because Mom really wants me to get better. I want to get better too, but I don't really understand better. I don't have a real feeling about who I would be then. If I was different, I know that would be better, though. I know that all this laying around and putting on all this weight is not better. I know that my head is sick still, even though the drugs keep me from thinking really bad thoughts. I know they are still in there though. I just don't listen to them or even hear them much anymore.

When I worked at Fed Ex, after I was a whiz but got fired, I got lost a lot. I got a job at Fed Ex because my Mom's brother, Uncle Marty, well, he had a big job there and he let me work with the guys. I didn't work there very long. I think I got lost too often and forgot to leave the packages. Doctor Mark said it was too soon. He said it put too much stress on me. That makes me sad because I liked that job. Mom told Uncle Marty she would drive with me and help, but that wasn't allowed. That would have been fun, though. We would have been a good team.

Mom comes home from work between five-thirty-five and five-forty-seven. When she comes home, on days when we're going to see Doctor Mark, then we go there. On days when we aren't going to see Doctor Mark, well, usually Mom will make something to eat, and then we eat it. Then, we talk or she reads and I watch TV or we stack dominoes on top of each other together. Sometimes she goes out and leaves me at home and sometimes we go out to eat at a restaurant, but not that often. Sometimes at night I turn off all the lights in the living room so no one can see into the house (I had Mom sit by the window and I went out into the street to check once, and all I saw was a shadow of her), and I look out the window and watch the cars and people go by. Sometimes Mom watches with me and she tells me where they are going and who they are. I try to figure it out too, but I'm just making things up. Mom says it's okay to pretend and that she doesn't really know who they are either, but I know she's only kidding me. No one could just make all that up.

When I get better I'm going to take Mom on a trip. We're going to go to a county fair and eat cotton candy and watch a rodeo like the ones I've seen on TV. When I get better we're going to drive places and look out a window that moves, where things go by because you are moving, not because they are moving past you but you are standing still. When I get better, I am going to be moving with everybody else instead of me, here, looking at them moving by outside my window. When I get better I'm going back to Fed Ex to work and drive my truck up people's streets and look in their windows as I go by. I just want to be that guy that drove by today. I just want to be him is all.

A Meditation

Should I light just the one candle or more... One seems so sad and lonely there by itself, I'll light two... more, maybe more than two, that might be too bright ... incense? That would add a peaceful mood... Yeah, why not? Where's the matches anyway? I haven't lit candles or incense for a while... Oh, under the magazine. Silence or one of those meditation tapes I just bought? The one with words of guidance or the nature sounds? I think nature sounds today... It's nice to have a choice. Okay, all set, I think I'll sit on the floor. Take some pillows from the couch and stack them here, and lean against the couch. I can't do that lotus position, no way! I'll just cross my legs. Oh crap, I forgot to turn the lights off and pull the curtains shut. Okay, all set now. Oh, set the alarm for, how long, maybe twenty minutes, or should I go for twenty-five? Twenty sounds about right... Not too long since I have to get going.

Breath, it's the concentration on the breath, in and out slowly, rhythmically, one two three four out, one two three four in, one two three out, one two three four oops, in one two three four, out one two three four—is four the right number of intakes and outtakes? It seems like I'm straining a bit to get to the fourth one, but I want to be breathing slowly, not coming close to hyperventilating or anything, just concentrate on slowly intaking and exhaling, slowly, what's the word, it's not intaking, it's… inhaling, that's it. It's funny with words how you can forget simple ones and how to spell them, or how all of a sudden they look so weird, ones that you know so well and use all the time. Maybe that happens a lot when you get old, you forget how to use and spell words, and they're always on the tip of your tongue, like they are sometimes now, but then it will be like that all the time. That will be really frustrating or maybe it won't be so frustrating if it happens constantly, you'll just get used to not remembering and that's just the way it is; you won't feel that you should know or remember it, which is how it is now. Now it doesn't happen that often so it irritates me and I have to go try to look up the word or else it just pops up in my head later in the day when I think I'm not thinking about it, but I must have done a brain search with some kind of find function and it took that long to find it or something, or else, why would I remember it that much later? The brain is so weird, how it works, we'll never be merged with computers like some people say. Computers can never think like our brains, I mean, they don't wonder about things, do they? They are just computing, not wandering and coming up with things randomly, which are usually the great things, like post-its was just a poorly sticking glue and look at it now, it was just an accident, like penicillin. That's when great things happen, accidentally. Artificial intelligence doesn't have accidents. It is just on-task. That's why our brains are so hard to study, the thought patterns are just so digressing, so stream of consciousnessy. How do you use that word as an adjective? Maybe you can't.

Anyway, my breathing is wrong again, one two three four out one two three four, in, out, slow, steady. Hmmmmm, that feels nice, kind of peaceful, inside somewhere. I wonder if it's working. Am I changing my body and mind connection right now? Am I slowing down my heart rate? It seems slower, I think. I think I'm really feeling that. It's hard to tell, actually, it's hard to just concentrate on the breath. Our brains are so active all day and then to just tell it, hey, slow down, smell the roses, take a load off, well, it's not used to that. Anyway, I think I'm getting it anyway, training myself to relax. It's good I'm doing this, but I need to do it every day, really, or else I won't get better at it. I need to give it momentum. Those yogis that have like twenty thousand hours of meditation have actually changed their brain waves. That would be great.

Should I close my eyes? I think I'm going to try it with eyes closed now. The color of the chair was distracting. I need to refinish it and it just reminds me and takes me out of my concentration on the breath. Yeah, eyes closed is better. Yeah, that's much better, that grayish peach inside of the eyes color. I can make out where the candles are, just a little bit more light there through my eyelids. They aren't very thick really, when you think about it. A lot of light comes through, they're like webbed feet, but on the eyes. Maybe they should be thicker so we could block out all the light from outside. I wonder if we would sleep better if we could close our eyes and be in total darkness instead of grayish-peach partial-darkness.

Oh, there's one of those weird eye patterns! I love those, but I can never make them stay. They are so fleeting and when you try to really see them and concentrate on the color and the patterns, they just immediately disappear. What are they called again, I remember I wrote it down from a college lecture once and I can never find that paper with the word, it starts with 'I' and it is long, like twelve letters or something. They are always lime green and chili red, hey, southwestern colors, with an endless number of patterns. Sometimes I would try to draw some and I would not be able to come up with too many designs and then I would try to make myself see them so that I could draw them, but if you really try they won't come, that's how they are. Plus, they are always moving so even if you could draw one, it just wouldn't capture the frenetic zigzaggy movements. But the imagination, well, it's not exactly imagination, it's whatever is going on in the rods and cones I think, anyway, that is much more creative than me sitting here, trying to draw them by willing them to be. There, I just had another one, with dashes and dots like Morse code or Braille or something. Cool. I wish I could see them whenever I wanted, like those 3-D pictures at dentists' offices where you have to strain and refocus your eyes for a few seconds and then the picture of the unicorn or whatever just appears.

Oh, my breathing's messed up again. God, it is really hard to just concentrate on that one thing without the mind just going every which way. Okay, I'm going to do it though, I don't care how hard it is. I can do it. Maybe next time I should listen to the tape with the words. This nature tape is too interesting. Is that a bird call? It doesn't sound like a bird, maybe a cricket. Or a frog, maybe. The birds in the yard don't sound like that. The chirps of the dove and the red-winged blackbird I can recognize, but most of the others just blend together. Maybe the birds on this tape are tropical birds, like in the Amazon. They wouldn't sound like birds here.

In one two three four, out one two three four, in one two three, out one two three, three seems more comfortable actually, four is pushing it. In one two three, out one two three, yeah, that's better. We've got to go camping again. Those sounds at night, asleep in the woods or by the beach, just a thin piece of material between us and the night, it's been too long. We just take nature for granted in the cities. There's no real interaction when you live in a house and keep the windows closed and the fan or air-conditioning on with all that noise and listen to the radio or TV and just don't have any connection to what's living right outside your door. It's so isolating. 'They' are out there and 'we' are in here. Like people who don't know any of their neighbors. The animals living outside are our neighbors but we don't know them either.

Now that's a frog, I'm sure. I want to buy one of those alarm clocks with the nature sounds so I can set the wake up to like whales or elephants or an ocean or something. The ocean might be too soothing and I wouldn't wake up. But then I could listen to them just when I fall asleep and wake up to the radio. I wonder if it would just be one of those gimmick things that I would never really use. It sounds like a good idea, but I've bought things that sounded good before and then never used them, like the foot massager or the pressed sandwich maker. I wish you could tell before you buy it if you really would use it. Just have a little snapshot into the future to see if it would fit in your life. Like, okay, I won't use that nature sounds function so that really expands my choices when I go buy an alarm clock.

Anyway, I'm off on my breathing again. One two three four, one two three four, one, oh, wait, I was going to just do three, but just now, a count of four seemed better. One two, three four, one two three four. Ahhhh, calm just washed over me. It's the control. It's forcing yourself to pay attention, be aware. Exerting some kind of order into your thoughts and body, the mind/body connection. Yeah, it's definitely working. I can feel it like a wave, washing across my brain, a calming flood. One two three four, one two three four. I'm really getting into it now, I can tell, it's just like the rainfall on the tape, clear little bell-like sounds, hitting a nerve somewhere within my brain, giving me shivers down my back and tingling somewhere on the back of my neck and into my scalp. This is great, it feels really relaxing. My brain is really quiet, I can tell. It's the combination of the counting the breaths and the chirping and the low background thunder and the grayish-apricot dark behind the lids and — BBBZZZZZZZ.

Is it twenty minutes already? It really flew by. Wow, I feel great, that was great. Meditation is so important. Ouch, my knees hurt from sitting—ouch, I need to remember to move my legs from now on. But that was so… I really need to do that more often, maybe every morning. I feel so refreshed. It's great to clear your head once in a while. I'm going to tell my friends to do it. I think it will really help all of us. I'm so glad I started this. God, is it eight o'clock already? I better get going. Shoot, I'm going to be late for work!

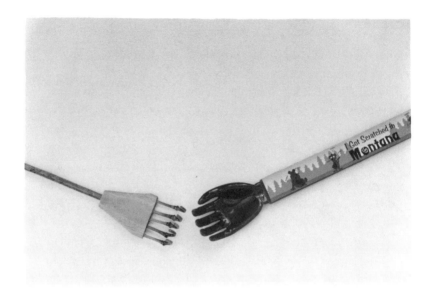

The Ghost of Christmas Presents

Call mine a cautionary tale.

I live in a Wal-Mart store in Lemon City, Florida during the holiday season. That's where I died, clutching a DVD player. They were on sale for $29 that morning, the day after Thanksgiving. Basically, I died for a DVD player, which in retrospect, doesn't seem worth it. But that morning, I might not have agreed. At 6am, there was a line down the block for the early-bird special: the first five hundred shoppers would receive a $15 gift certificate. If you do the math, that makes the DVD player $14. My sister and I didn't even bother to check around; we knew we wouldn't find it cheaper elsewhere.

It is always hard to determine actual numbers, like when the police say there were two thousand protestors and the protestors say there were ten thousand, but I'd say that there were close to five hundred people already there when my sister and I arrived. We were upset that we might miss out on the gift certificate, especially since we got up at 4:30 that morning, and we were pretty tired from all the work of Giving Thanks. I mean, we could have slept in until seven or so if we had known we wouldn't make the cut.

People were eyeing each other suspiciously in the line. When a Wal-Mart employee tried to cut across the line to get to work, they wouldn't move apart for her. They were counting in their heads to see what number they might be in line. People didn't speak to one another. It didn't seem very Christmas-cheery. They were shopping adversaries, as if about to compete in the Shopping Olympics, and no one wanted to give away any crucial bit of insider information through a slip of the tongue, like aisle location or where they could find something cheaper.

Right around Thanksgiving, this compulsion overtakes people. I know because I was one of them. The urge to buy everything that's on sale, whether the person you're buying it for will even want it, is a powerful one. If you don't buy it, someone will have something cheap that could have been yours if you had only shown more initiative. It didn't matter that I didn't know who I was going to give my DVD player to since my sister and I already had one. It was the deal that counted. My sister and I had planned a full day of shopping, with K-Mart the next stop, since there were certain items that were even cheaper there if you had a coupon and it was a 'blue light special', if I hadn't been trampled to death at the Wal-Mart first.

As soon as the Store Manager gave us the five-minute-warning over the megaphone, everyone in line snapped to attention. They adjusted the lacings on their shoes. They hoisted up their purses. They lifted children off the ground so they wouldn't slow them down. They hyperventilated. They waited like taut springs for the glass doors to inch apart. They shoved. They ran. They didn't care that there were elderly people in the line. They didn't notice anyone with disabilities. They wanted that DVD player and the gift certificate more than anything else in the world.

The first person to go down was an elderly man. He tripped and it was all over. No one stopped to help him. He was trampled. He cried out. Next to him, someone trying to avoid the fallen man ran into another man in a wheelchair and toppled it over. The toppler kept running toward the aisles. The man, now no longer in the wheelchair, tried to help the elderly man. He screamed for an employee to help them. The digital readout at the entrance of the store kept clicking out the number of people that had entered, the number rapidly approaching the magic five hundred mark. I watched in horror, as if seeing a train wreck coming but unable to stop myself from joining the rubbernecking throng. I could not have turned back even if I had wanted to at this point, as the momentum of the mob, which at this point felt like the mosh pit at a rock concert, was carrying me steadily toward the inevitable crush. I was beginning to panic. Someone next to me was elbowing me for my position. I looked over to see if it was my sister but it was a woman of about my age, staring at me with what could only be described as hatred. I couldn't catch my breath. I tried to convince myself to stay calm, but the crowd and the noise and the two men on the ground were creating an anxiety within me and I wondered what had happened to the spirit of Christmas. I wondered what had happened to civility and human kindness too, but just for a second. Because it was now my turn and the number on the wall read 493. I had made it! I didn't know where my sister was at that point since we had been separated by the crowd and I didn't care. I had my $15 gift certificate! I ran past the door with the others and sprinted toward the flashing red stop sign where the DVDs were. We all reached the DVDs together, pulling them off the pile like earthquake victims on a relief shipment. The last earthly thing I remember was that I had mine and was turning to get a cart to put it in when I was hit from behind by a falling box. It stopped me cold and I fell down, hitting my head on the DVD box rather than the floor, but still knocking me unconscious. I would have survived the initial head injury, but not the relentless trampling that followed as people stood on me to reach the higher boxes. I learned that the two men who had previously fallen had survived, although the elderly man had had a stroke during the melee and was not expected to walk or talk again. Most shoppers that day didn't know that anyone had been injured or died. When the paramedics finally arrived, those using me as a stepladder were oblivious to my existence.

I was taken to a hospital right on the ocean. It was a beautiful day. I died on the way to the hospital, but they kept trying to revive me anyway. I appreciate that they tried so hard, but they said that I was pretty young and had years of consumerism still in me and there was a chance that I could live with minimal brain damage if they could only make it through all the holiday shopping traffic and get me to the hospital.

Wal-Mart agreed to give my sister a free DVD player to replace the one that was pulled from under me as I lay unconscious. They said that they regretted the incident. They sent my sister a gift certificate even though she was number 509, and they let her keep mine. Wal-Mart said that it just showed how much consumer spending was up this year and happily quoted sales records for the week during the press conference about my untimely death.

Wal-Mart still offers incentives to shoppers to line up early and wait in line. Nothing changed with my death. I think for me, that was the hardest part of all. I know my sister was deeply affected by finding me under that pile of people and that her kids miss their aunt, especially around the holidays, but it's business as usual for everyone else.

That's why I haunt the Wal-Mart where I died as the *Ghost of Christmas Presents*. Since no one learned anything from my death I scare the crap out of them, hopeful that it'll remind them that they're lucky to be alive at all and that some of us get gypped. Fear is one of the few things that really seems to have some impact. I can't be here all year 'round since there's a lot to do elsewhere, but I get six weeks off at this time of year due to sympathy about my inconsequential demise to preach my gospel that there's more to the spirit of Christmas than lots of cheap stuff. And I try to prevent unnecessary carnage while I'm at it. I expect that seeing a ghost while you're shopping fundamentally changes the gist of the shopping experience. When I speak to the shoppers and remind them that I died for their sins, and that it really wasn't worth it, they run for the hills. I hope that it truly does some good besides the initial shock and they go back to their Wal-Mart-furnished homes and their Christmas trees and tinsel and ornaments and stockings and plastic wreaths and yule logs and nativity scenes with baby Santa Clauses and candy canes and lighted windows and fatty meats and excess and realize that someone tried to tell them something important that day. Someone tried to warn them that we are all getting trampled every day by our stuff. That Christmas is the time to appreciate, not appropriate. Remember loved ones past, not pass by someone else's passed-out loved one as she lies on the floor with a DVD player clutched under her, learning her lessons the good old-fashioned hard way.

Pacifist Chicken

In a card game up in Wetherspool back in '82 I won a chicken. Not the eatin' kind, see, this was a big pot with a lot ridin', and the chicken was worth somethin'. I didn't want it really, I had fightin' cocks, and I had some good studs, so this one was just another. Guy talked that bird up, what a killer he was, tough as nails, like that. And he had its papers to show and I just won it by accident. So he was mine and I took him home.

He was pretty enough, big enough, seemed to have some fire, but I had no idea what was comin' to me.

I put them papers away and I put him out with the others. He settled in, and I plum forgot about him. A few days later a guy comes for a fighter and I talked up this chicken cause I didn't need him and I sold him this bird for a good price. He took off with him and I expected to never see that bird again.

Few days pass and the man comes back, carryin' the cock. He

don't want him no more, sure wants his money though. See, the bird don't want to fight. No sir. He said it was the damndest thing. The bird ducked the fight all right, and tired out the other and well, he wanted a fighter. "Wait," says I, "he won cause the other one tired out?"

"I guess, but it weren't much to watch," says he. Guess not. What could I do but give him his money back and watch him drive away down the gravel road, me chewin' his grit and dust. I coughed, looked at the bird. He seemed all right, so I put him back in the pen with them others.

Happens again, just the same. I sold him off, hopin' it was a one time thing, but back he comes to me. And this one was madder than the first. Cussin' me and the bird, woulda killed and ate it if he didn't want his money more, he says. No tellin'.

Now I'm gettin' curious myself. I put him in with one of my bruisers, just us, no lookies, just to see. Damn straight, but that bird don't want to fight no how. He ducks and backs off and skirts like a prizefighter sparrin' with a fool. When my Dude starts to go down for tiredness, this other, now I'm callin' him Shoegum cause I can't lose him, this Shoegum just sits down, dainty as you please. Well, Dude sees that as weak and goes for him hard but Shoegum moves out of the way and sits down again. It went on like that for a spell, but I'm seein' a goldmine. This is new, real new. And I think I'm lookin' at my retirement.

I been thinkin' about this for long and hard. It's no business for a man of my year and grey head and swoll up fingers. And I seen too much blood and shootin' and cussin' and maulin' and innards and ugliness and I want to sit on my chair and do just that, sit. Stare at nothin' if I feel like it all day. Stare at a bird that ain't about to fight or get fought. Maybe a robin or a damn sparrow for Christ's sake. But I ain't quite got enough. They say that you always say you ain't got quite enough no matter how much you got, but I know that I ain't got quite enough for real. I did some figurin' on a piece of paper upstairs and I need some more so's I don't have to see every hole in my sock and be thinkin' I have to live with it cause I ain't got enough.

A hole in the sock can get to a man like that. Make him keep thinkin' he ain't never gonna have enough.

So I look again at Shoegum and I look at him square. He don't look special, not really. He's blue mostly, some yellow and red on the neck, about average size for a fightin' male, 'cept he ain't fightin'. He don't look smarter than them others, don't look bright no how. Don't even seem to be thinkin' at all.

I set up some action with some friends of mine. I don't do this much. I breed and sell 'em, go to the fights, but I don't get in on fights. But now I say I got somethin' extra and I want to try him out. They don't ask no questions, give me a round. I don't like to bet neither. But I do on this one, not much, just in case he foolin' me. So, it's a small gatherin' back behind Jake Sturgis' barn away from the roadside. Them people from the animal welfare society been actin' up and we got to be more careful than before. Don't need no trouble from no society. Never used to have no trouble. Things are changin' no doubt when you gotta hide from your neighbors. Most of these guys didn't even know chickens was animals, had to be told.

It's the regulars. There's about thirty of us, locals who are in the business or in the business of watchin' and bettin'. Sometimes somebody'll bring someone new, here and there, but mostly you know who'll be there. Tonight there's about twelve, fifteen of 'em. About usual. Crawford, he brings Cuba, he's the colors of the Cuban flag he says, which are the same damn colors as the American flag but he don't call him Patriot or America, and there ain't much blue on him at all, but he's a tough fighter and for a spell, I'm not so sure. Crawford asks what I got to show but I ain't talkin'. I say he'll see like the rest of 'em. And me too, I think, but I don't let on.

Cuba's a strutter and lookin' for comers. Shoegum comes out of his box cool as you please, not even payin' Cuba a look. Cuba arches and scrapes and looks ready. Shoegum looks sleepy, his eyes half closed. Crawford looks at me and then at Shoegum and back to me. "You gonna fight with that?" I nod. "I ain't responsible," he says.

"I know," I says. "Me neither."

That riles him. "Fine," he says. "Let's do it then." My knees are weak as I sit. Why am I so nervous? If he loses, well, so that's God's plan. One less chicken in the world, and a little harder and longer I got to work.

Shoegum don't seem to be risin' to the fight at all. I hear some grumbles and whispers and some are lookin' at me. I know they're thinkin' I'm gettin' old and maybe I don't have no sense no how. Maybe I don't know a fighter no more. Maybe I don't know nothin'. Maybe it's time for new blood in the breedin' business, but I act like I don't notice. Cause I ain't so sure they ain't right. It all seems kinda wrong, outta whack, a cock that won't fight, a fightin' cock that don't want no part of it. Anyway, I'm in it now and that's it. So I watch like the rest of 'em.

Crawford takes Cuba out of his cage and holds him tight since he's strainin' under his want to fight. I hold Shoegum the same, actin' like he needs the restrainin' when it must be pretty clear that he don't. He's pokin' at his backside the whole time, like he's got a itch that's more important than Jesus. I'm gettin' worse nervous, thinkin' I made a big mistake when the bell rings and we have to let 'em at each other. What can I do, I give a little prayer to myself and touch him like it's the last time, and let him go.

Well, he looks over at Cuba and Cuba don't waste no time lookin' and charges. Shoegum manages to avoid him and skirts to the corner. Cuba is fast and quick and mean and I'm lookin' at Shoegum with pure pity and so's the rest of 'em, but he just keeps dodgin' and weavin' and skirtin' and doin' a damn good job of not fightin'. I look around the crowd that has moved in on the fight. They look confounded. I shrug my shoulders at the looks, look back at Shoegum. He sits down. Damn the sounds that come from the crowd. They ain't never seen that before.

He don't sit long, cause Cuba's on him right quick, but he sits again first chance. And it sure does seem that Cuba's easin' off of him, not givin' it near all he could. Shoegum seems to have taken the fight out of Cuba, which ain't happened before neither. Cuba don't do that.

Cuba struts around a while, lookin' at Shoegum, figurin' out what's up. He don't know any more than the rest of us, but with Shoegum seated and pullin' at some feathers on his neck, lookin' like a sittin' duck in any other damn fight, Cuba just sits hisself down too and starts pullin' at his own feathers.

"What the hell!" Storms Crawford. "God damn bird get out there and kick his ass."

Cuba don't do it. He don't do nothin'. Crawford picks the bird up and throws him at Shoegum. Shoegum dodges Cuba and the bird walks to the other side, away from Crawford. There's a dumbstruck pause.

"Winner, Shoegum!" shouts Jake.

"Anybody want a bird?" Crawford asks the crowd, speakin' of Cuba. He walks away from the ring and the fight and leaves Cuba in there. I pick Shoegum up and put him in his box. Cuba walks over to the box and looks in at Shoegum. I pick up Cuba and put him in his own box and stack 'em one atop the other and start to leave.

"Whoa there old timer," I hear. I turn. Jake's handin' me some money. My winnings.

"What you got there?" he asks strangely.

"I got me a rockin' chair and a cold beer and a view of the back hills," I says. He don't know what I mean I'm sure, but he nods. I get a few more of those looks like I'm losin' what mind I had, and I figure I better get goin'.

Jake comes by the next day with a bird doctor he knows. The doctor was at the fight. Jake says he ain't seen nothin' like it before, in all his years at it. "Can he do it again?"

"I guess so," I says. We walk to the yard and Shoegum and Cuba are walkin' together, Shoegum leadin', Cuba followin'.

"Damn," says Jake. "Ain't seen nothin' like it," he repeats.

The bird doctor keeps watchin' too. "It ain't natural," he says.

"I know," I says. "What you think?"

The doctor looks back to me, real serious like. "I think you got to try him again. And again. You might have somethin' big here. You might have somethin' real rare, a bird that can influence other birds. Not that I've seen that before. Cause it just ain't natural." Cuba is groomin' Shoegum. Shoegum stands quietly for it.

"You got to make you some money with this here bird," says Jake.

"I aim to," I says. The doctor shakes his head. The doctor and Jake leave, Jake sayin' he'll fix me another fight.

That night I had a dream, a crazy drunken dream only I was sober. Well, I'd had one before bed, but that ain't nothin' to speak of. Shoegum was a holy bird. He had followers, bird and man alike, and he was, by example showin' them about not fightin'. About turnin' the other cheek. And he was preachin' the word by goin' into that ring and bringin' them birds down by not doin' his job. By showin' them the way of layin' down. And people started givin' him coins and gifts and food and cloth and jewelry and lookin' to him to heal them. He didn't seem to understand none of it, but he *was* it. That's it, he just was this thing. I could speak for him, so I would say, his holiness say you got to go home and eat more carrots, or his holiness want you to stop hittin' your kids, or his holiness say you need to make peace with your neighbor.

So I stopped puttin' him in the ring and set him up like the holy bird he was and people started comin' from all around, bringin' their ills and it was gettin' out of hand. They wanted to touch him and pull at his feathers and he was tired. Plain wore out from all the attention and effort. I was worried about him so I set up hours they could come, but he was gettin' weak. One day he up and died, just leaned over and sighed and he left this place, peaceful like.

I woke up ballin' like a baby over Shoegum and ran out to see him. He was just fine out there in the pen, out in the light of a new moon and I felt better and climbed back into bed and shivered and wondered what the hell this was all about.

But it all started to come true. I took him to other fights and his reputation as a bird that could win by not fightin' was too temptin' for most of these folks to resist. They was bringin' their best cocks, big and mean and ugly and they left cowed and aged a few years after a round with Shoegum. I started thinkin' I should give him a more dignified name, like King or Highness, but by then everyone knew him as Shoegum so what could I do. Shoegum kept winnin' by losin' and a coupla times I was scared one of these guys would try to hurt him or me on account of how mad they were for losin' this way. And I was makin' some money and I bought Shoegum some fancy organic feed, the best I could find, and gave him his own cage for when he wanted to be by hisself.

Some guy from the city heard about Shoegum and he came out to do a story on him for the paper. He went to a fight and it was a good one to see cause Shoegum was gettin' quick at endin' these things with even the toughest bird and he wasn't waitin' to tire 'em out so much no more, he was almost like hypnotizin' 'em, takin' the fight out of 'em early, makin' 'em see the wrong in it. Well, it was in the paper the next day and we all got scared that them society people was gonna come down on us so we laid low for a while, but the people started to come to see Shoegum anyway.

So I put up a sign down the road a piece sayin' SPECIAL CHICKEN WITH POWERS and they found me, them that knew. I put some ribbons in his cage and fancied him up with a bell on his foot. And they brought beads and coins and all, like in the dream, and they prayed to him and touched him and he put up with it. I was worried that he might peck someone, you never know, and then I felt bad for thinkin' that, since he was a special chicken with powers, and wouldn't peck to save his own skin. And I didn't think he'd peck a hand that only wanted to touch him so's he could heal 'em, even though I wasn't so sure about the healin' part, but belief can be a powerful thing, so's I didn't want to interfere.

Most days there was a line to see him. Cars was parked all over my yard, and I didn't know what to do with these folks. They was arguin' and sometimes pushin' to get a look at him. Fifty cents for a look, two dollars to touch him. I was cleanin' up. Some people was freethinkers, some not believin' at all, but somebody had told 'em and they told somebody and on it goes. I even had some other newspaper folks and a call about the TV, but I wasn't sure that was a good idea. I didn't think Shoegum would want to be on the TV.

Now cock fightin' was at a real low in town and some folks

wasn't so happy about that. Others were real happy, and thought that Shoegum could be some kinda savior and wanted me to set up a church for him and I thought that was plain loco, but I was scared that somebody might try to kill or steal him. He was bad for business for the unconverted you could say. Some folks just thought I had trained him funny, in my spare time, found a way to make him turn those other cocks yellow. Now how would I do that I wondered but I might think the same thing myself since it's so damn strange, even to me.

One day who shows up but the guy I won Shoegum from in the card game. He looks me over and says "You a damn fraud. I know that bird and he ain't no holy bird, he's just plain yellow and dumb as can be." He had them papers and that's true, he says, but he was just a case of good seed gone bad. "I knew I was cheatin' you and I felt kinda bad about it, but now you cheatin' all these people and when I heard about it, I had to come and let you know that I know and you can't get away with it. You makin' them believe and there ain't nothin' to believe in at all, just a feather and bones faker, like yourself."

"Now you hold on," says I. "Have you been to one of his fights?"

"Are you a fool," says he. "Of course, that's why I was lookin' to dump him myself."

"I'm talkin' 'bout since you unloaded him on me?" I asked.

"I don't have to," says he "since I known that bird since he was born and he ain't nothin' special. I would know."

"You don't know nothin'," says I and I was gettin' riled since Shoegum didn't have to prove hisself to no card cheatin' doubter. "He ain't fightin' no more anyway," says I, "cause he got a followin' and he's retired, just preachin' the word of peace."

"Bunkum," says the card cheat. "I gonna stop you from makin' fools of them folks," says he, with a backward look, and stomps off my property. Now I never seen it before, not on nobody, but I got the willies from that bum what raised Shoegum, and damned if he ain't got a evil eye, I thinks to myself. I washed my hands good after he left and tried to put him right outta my mind, but it weren't so easy.

That night there was a terrible powerful rain. I ran out when I seen it comin' with a bit of tin for a roof for Shoegum and covered his cage. The ribbons were already soggy and not so pretty no more by the time I got there. Shoegum was wet but he seemed okay and I made up my mind right then that when the rain stopped I was gonna let him come live in the house with me and bring him out only for the show times. I knew this was crazy talk, crazy as can be, but he was in my blood now, like kin and I felt responsible for him. I didn't sleep too good that night, the rain thrashin' hard against my place, and when the sun come up and I heard the crowin' I jumped up hard and fast for a man my age. When I got to the cage, it was bad. Puddles had formed around it and Shoegum didn't look good at all. He was pantin' all wrong and not standin' right. I got so scared I shook and scooped him up and brought him into my bed right quick. I tucked him under my covers and brought him his special feed that he got all over my blankets but I didn't care at all. But he didn't even notice the food. He just lay there.

I called that bird doctor and told him to get out there quick cause Shoegum needed him. I told the folks wantin' to see him that he was takin' a few days off to rest since all the healin' and peace givin' had given him a turn for the worse. They were none too happy about this since some said they come from as far away as a hundred miles, but I told 'em to see the sights and come back in a few days. The doctor came then and he said right off it don't look good for Shoegum. I choked back a sob right there and said, "Doc you gotta save him. You know he ain't just a cock fightin' chicken damn it. He's changed people's and chicken's lives. He's got more good to do."

"I know," says the doc, but he don't hold no store by his cures. He says Shoegum got some kinda alien flu and it's goin' around and it ain't good. Says he's seen it kill a bird in a few days.

"What can I do?" I cried. "He's all I got." He gave me some medicine and told me to give it to him by dropper if he wouldn't take it with food and to keep him dry and wait and see. I didn't know if I could wait and see I was jumpy as a skunk. I hovered over that bird like he was the queena sheeba and any little crow or choke or movement and I ran over and pulled up the covers and patted his head. He didn't seem to be doin' no better the next day so I called the doc again. He said he wouldn't come out 'cause there was nothin' he could do. Wait and see he says.

I lay in the bed with Shoegum that night, right next to him, scared I might roll over on him so's I couldn't sleep. In the night he was makin' an awful racket and all I could think of was the death rattle and I started to cry and moan myself. I stroked his head and talked to him and I prayed for him I swear I did pray for that chicken. I said to God that I didn't care about the money I'd give it all back and I would never breed another bird to fight and I would pray every day to him if he would save my Shoegum. Shoegum rattled on and as long as he was breathin' I knew he weren't dead yet. This went on all night until near dawn I finally fell asleep.

I woke late in the mornin' and Shoegum weren't in the bed with me. I cried out and jumped from the bed and looked under it scared he had falled off in the night and broke his neck, but he weren't there. I looked everywhere but couldn't find him. Finally, in the kitchen I found him on the counter, peckin' at a bit of seed that spilled there. Overjoyed with joy, I ran to him and tried to hold him and stroke him but he ducked away from me and jumped to the floor. I put a mess of feed in a bowl and watched with pure happiness while he ate it all down and looked up for more. I gave him as much as he could hold and then tried to pet him again and this time I got the shock of my life when he pecked at my hand. It drew blood. I stared at the blood like I ain't never seen my own blood before. Shoegum ain't never even tried to do nothin' like that before. I talked to him, said he must still not be hisself. Maybe he needs to go out I think so I opened the door and let him into the yard.

Out he goes to the pen. I opened the gate and let him in and Cuba and some of the others run over, happy to see him it sure looks like, and he does the damndest thing. He lunges for Cuba and takes a piece out of his wing. Cuba leaps back so surprised and hurt that I near feel sorry for him. What the hell? I think. Shoegum struts over to his cage and goes in and I go back to the house and sit down at the table and I just sit there. For a long time.

Is this what you give me lord, you give me my Shoegum back but it ain't Shoegum no more? I know I weren't no saint, but I musta sure done some wrongs to you to hurt me like this. I thought if somebody were near death that they come back changed better, thankful 'bout havin' a second chance and all that. What did it do to Shoegum but make him mean and ugly when he weren't that way before. You might as well have just taken him from me, that would be better than seein' him like this. He ain't no better than any other bird now, not special at all.

Then I hear a racket outside and I run out and I see Shoegum goin' after Cuba like it's the fight of his life. I jump in like a crazy man to break it up and I see Shoegum tryin' to give it all he got to poor Cuba and then I see the glory. Cuba won't fight him. He be dodgin' and weavin' hisself now. He learnt from the master and now he's givin' it all right back. Them other chickens in the pen come right over, gettin' in Shoegum's way, blockin' his charges. They's a mighty team, all against the one. When it seems that Shoegum's beat, Cuba sits hisself down, tendin' to his wound. Damn if it ain't just the way it went before, but different.

Somebody pulled in to see him just then and I stood up and shooed 'em away, sayin' Shoegum had some powerful black magic and couldn't see nobody no how. I went in the house and wrote a sign sayin' CLOSED and hung it on the fence.

And I stood by that fence and I watched the goin's on in that pen and remembered the first time I seen Shoegum not fight and I thought I don't know nothin' 'bout nothin'.

But somebody does.

What Did You Expect?

I expected that I would be happier by now. I expected to be married with a few kids. I expected it to be easier. I expected to know more. I expected to have greater personal satisfaction in my job since now I know what I'm doing. I thought I would have more time to do things I wanted. I expected to be more connected to my neighbors and my community. I never thought time would go so fast or that I would say that. I expected that I would have gotten through a lot of these issues and not still be so stuck. I thought you just automatically bonded with your kid. I thought I would make more money with my photography. I expected to be living a less conventional life. I didn't think I would become so cynical and passionless. I never thought I would need Viagra in a million years. I expected to be married for the rest of my life. I never used to worry about my weight or looking young. I thought I would have deeper friendships. I didn't think that regular drinking would turn me into an alcoholic. I expected that if I got an advanced degree I would never have trouble finding a job. I thought the stock market would keep on going up and up. I never thought I could have such strong negative feelings toward the mother of my children. I expected that everyone felt like I did. I didn't know it would cost so much just to get by. I'd always hoped to be an expert on Something. I thought that trip to India for three months would profoundly change me. I thought that if I denied myself pleasure I would feel more connected to god. I thought once I found someone to be with who wanted to be with me, that things would just fall into place. My wedding will be the happiest day of my life. I thought she loved me. I think this time he's really going to leave his wife. I expected to have a better relationship with my parents as I got older. I thought I would like being an event planner. I thought when you confided in someone that it was sacred. I thought doing the weeklong relationship retreat would save our marriage. I thought that collecting pre-Columbian art would give me more long-term satisfaction. I thought that breaking into the film business wouldn't be hard if you had talent. I thought the movie would be good since it got a 'thumbs up'. I don't believe that everyone is for sale. I just thought there would be more meaning. I hope he notices me today. I thought if you got a dog it attracts chicks. I generally don't have much luck with blind dates. I thought she was using birth control. I have no idea why I'm not rich. I thought therapy would fix me. Believe me, I've learned my lesson this time. I thought taking vitamins was a bunch of crap. I expected to have my own business by now. I believe that the USDA stamp means our meat is safe. I thought once my kids grew up I wouldn't have to worry about them anymore. We knew it was hurricane season, but our travel agent said they were really rare. I just wish things were different. I'm really tired of hearing about the good old days. Of course I vote—every single one counts. I thought AIDS happened to other people. I don't believe in karma because it's a dog-eat-dog world out there and you have to do whatever it takes to survive. Should we bring the gun? I just want to fall in love. Why didn't you call? Pretend I never said it. I thought that whitening my teeth would change my whole look. For that much money, I expected it to last longer. We didn't think we would be constantly fighting about the wedding. I'm reading that *Never Be Lied To Again* book. Running a household is a twenty-four-hour-a-day job. I used to believe that people were basically good, but now I'm not so sure. I guess I should have taken better care of myself. Nobody tells you this stuff. Breast implants are safe. Don't worry, someone else will take care of that. I took that new diet drug and lost a bunch of weight … then I gained it all back. I was disappointed by the great pyramids; they were so small. Don't worry; you can't miss it! There'd be some kind of investigation if our intelligence really knew in advance. I thought they said there was an imminent threat to this country. I need to live in a gated community to feel safe. Do we have to wait in line? I'm hoping if I change he'll love me more. She's so moody I never know who I'm dealing with. I've been meeting so many losers on match.com. Of course you're harassed if you disagree; that's what makes this a free country! I wish I wasn't so busy, because I'd like more peace in my life. I know we wanted to get away from it all, but there are no good restaurants here and I can't get cell phone reception. All I need is a vacation to feel refreshed again. My agent never returns my phone calls. It would be so great to be a celebrity. I have a hard time working freelance because I never know when I'll have a job. You're not getting older, you're getting better. My 40th was the worst birthday I ever had. You can prolong your youthful appearance with regular facial peels. I think that global warming is greatly exaggerated. They indoctrinate you young with wishing on a star and blowing out the candles on your birthday cake and throwing coins in a fountain and pretty soon you believe dreams come true. I definitely believe in a hell. I'm not insecure but I'm looking into penile enlargement. They're finding new species all the time, so the ones that we're losing are being replaced. I can't afford car insurance. I used to hate cell phones in public, but now that I have one, I don't mind. He cheated on his third wife on their honeymoon. I just thought I would feel something when he finally died. If it doesn't work out we can always sell it. Can you find a date for my buddy?

For *that* you have to register as a sex offender? When I get that promotion, I'll finally have enough to live comfortably on. Poor people should just move out of those bad neighborhoods. I'm just waiting for my big break! If you loved me you would. I think driving a Mercedes says 'I've made it.' I feel safe in a big car. I can quit on my own, I don't need to join any self-help group. I've tried to quit smoking, but I'm just too addicted. Why do kids always want to do things they're told not to? I kissed a guy with a split tongue and it grossed me out. I don't do pro-bono work, it takes up too much of my time. They said it was painless. I don't like having pets; they always die. I hope my next life doesn't seem this ephemeral. I expect our government to respond with force to an implied threat to this country. I thought I would be better in a crisis. I'm too busy at work to look for a new job. I think kids will really complete us. My kids love to watch professional wrestling. We're looking at buying an old fixer-upper. I know she's eighty, but my Mom is so out of touch with what's going on today. I didn't think that I would always be so tired. Isn't there a shortcut? Now that I've finally made my first million it just doesn't seem like that much anymore. I don't have kids so why should *my* property taxes go to the schools? Let's just worry about that later. Rolfing is supposed to get rid of cellulite forever. So, you're going to ask her to marry you on TV? I thought we lived in a civilized society. I thought my kids would take care of me when I was this age. We'll go one of these days, I promise. I should have never bought him that kazoo. I thought since everybody did it that it wasn't actually illegal. I think the Palestinians and Israelis should just sit down and work out their differences. No strings attached? I'm too overweight to exercise. Is this all there is? I expected to be more appreciated. I wonder why all the executives in this company dress the same. Yeah, if I looked like him I'd have a lot of dates too. I know it doesn't seem like it, but I think she really loves me. I don't want to live at this nursing home; it's full of old people. Didn't you want me to remind you of something? The food was better in Paris. I thought I would never date an ugly guy. I know I'm obese, but that doesn't keep me from doing anything a thin person can do. I can have sex with a lot of guys since it doesn't mean anything to me. My broker says advertising keeps this economy going. I know I don't need it, but I want it. Is that real pleather? It's just a matter of time 'til I make it as an actor. Well, I didn't know they were poisonous when I ate them, of course! It was weird when I realized that my dad wasn't always right. I can't wear sapphires; they're not my birthstone. These stiletto heels are killing my feet. Let's just move on, the holocaust was over fifty years ago; that could never happen again! Our nuclear secrets are very well protected. Terrorists need to really think about what they're doing to this world. It's always the quiet loner types. I've never won anything in my life. I don't mind staying late at work because I think they really notice. I can't believe even my small breasts are starting to sag. I really do hope there is a god. If I care, I always get hurt. I wonder what it would be like to be with a twenty year-old guy again? I'm looking for someone with a lot of money. I just want it to be perfect, that's all. I know myself and I can only learn the hard way. I know my life's a mess, what do you want me to do? I wish I was, or is it were, smarter. I tried to run for office, but I have a really bad memory. I don't have time to read for pleasure. I've got plenty of time, I'm only thirty. Yes, I'm a spiritual person, I mean, I'm a Catholic. Peace marching really sends a message to the White House. Those protests in Seattle changed everything. If I listen to my inner-child I feel like throwing a temper tantrum. I didn't expect to feel so lonely after my dog died. Do you like my painting? I thought we needed chemicals to control the bugs, but now everything is dead. Budgeting is for cheap people. I thought that Prozac would make me happy. It seems like I just got here. Promise you'll never lie to me. I thought he would love a surprise party. I never thought I would be an angry man like my father. Well, I'm never going to be like that when I get old! Space travel should be perfected by now. My driver's license picture is horrible. I knew he was The One the moment I saw him. I thought we would always have that passion between us like that first year. I thought you could make someone love you. It's just not fair! I expected more kindness from my fellow human beings. I hoped meditation would lead me to enlightenment.

I'm sure it'll be easy! Would you tell me if you thought I was misguided? One day it will all be over. And *then* I get the free trip to Florida? I knew it was too good to be true. We really need to look at Communism as a viable system in this country. We just need to take the money out of politics. I wish somebody would die and leave me a million dollars. I'm too avant-garde for the commercial filmmaking business. I knew it was cheap but I still thought it would be good. Virtual reality isn't really that much like reality actually. Maybe I should stop throwing myself at him. I will for the rest of my life, I mean I do. Why me, god? When I'm depressed, eating a lot makes me feel better, until it doesn't. It'll just be for a few months, I promise. I had hoped my family would be more supportive. I stopped believing in psychics after 9-11. Why do they hate us—we're the most generous country on the planet. I thought having a cat would be less of a commitment. I never see my friends that have children anymore. Why didn't somebody tell me having a kid was so much work? I don't think I'm contagious any more. Isn't my girlfriend beautiful? I thought I wouldn't really notice the age difference. I love you. I thought we were friends. Thinking about dying is depressing. I don't have to write it down, I'll remember. I got such a bad sunburn in Cancun last August. I expect to get cancer. I thought it was impossible to have a cover up on that massive of a scale. I thought our government was there to protect us, its citizens. I didn't think airport security would really take my scissors. You really have to know somebody in this business. But I always cleaned the needle when I used to shoot up! I thought he really meant it. No wonder the printers are so cheap; they kill you on the ink jet cartridges. I didn't think I'd have to take computer programming classes just to use my PC. Now that you know them, stop pushing my buttons! Do I look fat in this? Could I be a vegetarian but still eat meat sometimes? Maybe there's something to that mind/body connection. It was just a one-night thing; it will never happen again. Anytime something's too hyped, I tend to be disappointed by it. I thought it said 'free'. Quick, knock on wood! I've tried fasting but I just got too hungry. I'm sure those lynxes in my coat were trapped humanely—it's a Versace after all. I'd rather not know anything bad. You can learn a lot watching TV. I try to do the right thing, but it isn't easy. I had high hopes for a better world. It really hurt my feelings that nobody believed me when I was abducted by aliens. I guess we should have read the instructions. I don't know why people get so upset by practical jokes. There's always next year. My doctor stopped making house calls. I know we hardly knew each other, but I had no idea she was doing drugs. I thought we decided we weren't going to be late anymore. I know I'm taking chances, but I really like to drive fast. Why do bad things happen to good people? Maybe it's not dead. I thought we repaired that hole in the ozone layer last year. I want to get a tattoo, but not because my friends all have them; I want mine to be different. It seems like all politicians only care about getting reelected. I guess I was just surprised that the stuff I learned in physics works in the real world. He was really mean to me after I dumped him. It was the floor model. I'd love to eat organic food, but it's more expensive. Capitalism isn't all it's cracked up to be. Why can't we all just get along? I can't handle alcohol like I used to. I never thought I'd love my kid more than my dog. They just want us all too busy working keeping the economy going to question why we're doing it. That crying baby is driving me crazy. I told you we should never have moved next door to the Parks and Recreation Department's heavy equipment yard. Why does he keep asking *why* all the time? I thought I could handle the stress. Working in customer service is very trying. I knew there had to be a gimmick. I think I'm just vaguely dissatisfied with my options. What do you mean it's past the warranty period? That modern art show was just too out there for me. It looked better in the picture. Why is everybody so crabby? Doesn't it come with that? I thought the rapture would happen last weekend. We're doomed. And then one day there was no more new car smell.

Photo by Teness Herman

After completing her Masters Degree in Film Writing and Production from Columbia College in Chicago, Andrea Kampic worked in Hollywood as a still photographer, camera assistant, and second unit film director while writing screenplays.

In *Pacifist Chicken*, Andrea sets free the insightful, cutting prose she honed while earning a degree in journalism from the University of Wisconsin, Madison. She distills her quirky observations into smile-think-laugh-think again stories that ask you to question your expectations and hopes since *they* may be doing the driving and you are just along for the ride.

This is her first book. She lives in Los Angeles in a love shack by the river with her longtime boyfriend Brian and their family of animals.